Kat was feeling vulnerable, and she knew she was in danger of falling for Oliver's charm.

He created an energy around him, around her.

Oliver kept a slight distance between them as they walked outside, but even so she was still aware of a field of attraction and desire surrounding them. Or at least, surrounding her.

She turned toward him as they stopped at her car.

"I'll see you at work," he said as he opened the door that she'd once again left unlocked. "And I'm looking forward to our date," he added. "But, until then," he said as he bent his head and leaned toward her.

Kat didn't intend to but she lifted her face, angling it up to him.

Was he going to kiss her?

Her eyelids drifted down, half-closed.

She could feel his breath on her skin and then his lips pressed against her cheek, just in front of her ear, briefly touching her. Too briefly.

Dear Reader,

Coober Pedy in South Australia is an amazing place. It is famous for its opals but, over the years, numerous movies have been filmed there, too, so that's where I decided to send my Hollywood playboy when he needed to stay out of trouble. Where better than the middle of nowhere—the Australian outback?

But, when it turns out that Coober Pedy isn't far enough away and Oliver finds himself in trouble once again, Kat is the person he turns to for help. A gorgeous, sensible paramedic, born and bred in the outback, she should know better than to fall for a movie star, but Oliver is nothing if not charming!

To Damien, Dean and Roger—thank you for showing me your town and for lending me your names. And to Dave Reed—I hope you enjoy seeing your name in a romance novel!

I had fun with my characters and I had a lot of fun trying to capture Coober Pedy on the page. If you'd like to see some photos of my trip you can visit my Facebook page, Facebook.com/emily.forbes.5855.

Best wishes,

Emily

TAMING HER
HOLLYWOOD PLAYBOY

———

EMILY FORBES

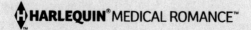
HARLEQUIN® MEDICAL ROMANCE™

Recycling programs
for this product may
not exist in your area.

ISBN-13: 978-1-335-64200-4

Taming Her Hollywood Playboy

First North American Publication 2019

Copyright © 2019 by Emily Forbes

Printed in U.S.A.

Books by Emily Forbes

Harlequin Medical Romance

The Christmas Swap
Waking Up to Dr. Gorgeous

The Hollywood Hills Clinic
Falling for the Single Dad

Tempted & Tamed
A Doctor by Day…
Tamed by the Renegade
A Mother to Make a Family

A Kiss to Melt Her Heart
His Little Christmas Miracle
A Love Against All Odds
One Night That Changed Her Life
Falling for His Best Friend
Rescued by the Single Dad

Visit the Author Profile page
at Harlequin.com for more titles.

For Deb,
the most amazing big sister.
I was so lucky to have you in my life.
I miss you every day.
xx
6th October 2018

**Praise for
Emily Forbes**

"*A Mother to Make a Family* is a lovely story about
second chances with life and love…. A well written,
solid tale of sweet love and charming family."
—*Goodreads*

PROLOGUE

'*Toto... I've a feeling we're not in Kansas any more.*'

The familiar phrase from *The Wizard of Oz* popped into Oliver's head as he sat in the all-terrain vehicle surrounded by nothing but red dirt. The heat in the vehicle was stifling but he knew it was worse outside. He could see the shimmering mirage of the heat as it rose off the baked land. A trickle of sweat made its way down his back, sliding between his shoulder blades as he looked out of the window and wondered what he was doing at the end of the earth.

He wasn't in Kansas, and he sure as heck wasn't in Hollywood either. Hollywood was clean and tidy, ordered and structured. A lot of the work on movie sets in today's world was done indoors, with air-conditioning and green screens, and any dirt, gore, murders, blood and disasters were manufactured. Here the dirt and dust and heat were all too real. Too authentic. It made him wonder about everything else—the murders, blood and disasters—it was too easy to imagine all kinds of skulduggery occurring in this seemingly endless land.

He shrugged his shoulders; they were sticky under his clothing as he returned his focus to the task at hand. He'd always had an active imagination but he was sure he'd be able to handle this place—it was only for six weeks. The dirt and dust would wash off at the end of the day, he was used to a certain level of discomfort in his job, and he certainly wasn't precious—although the heat was a little extreme, even for him. It had a thickness to it which made breathing difficult, as though the heat had sucked all the oxygen from the air. It felt like the type of heat you needed to have been born into, to have grown up in, to have any chance of coping with it. Of surviving.

It must have been well over one hundred degrees in the shade, if there was any shade. The place was baking. Hot, dry and not a blade of grass or a tree in sight to break the monotony of the red earth. The landscape was perfect for the movie but not so great for the cast and crew. Adding to Oliver's discomfort was the fact that he was wearing a flame-retardant suit under his costume in preparation for the upcoming scene. But it was no use complaining: he asked to do his own stunt work wherever possible and he was sure his stunt double would be more than happy to sit this one out.

The sun was low in the sky but the heat of the day was still intense. He closed his eyes as he pictured himself diving into the hotel pool and emerging, cool and fresh and wet—instead of hot and sticky and dripping in sweat—to down a cold beer. He would love to think he could have the pool to himself but he knew, in this overwhelming climate, that was wishful thinking; he'd just have to do his best to avoid sharing it with any of the single women from the cast or crew. He didn't need any more scandals attached to his name. His agent, lawyer and publicist were all working overtime as it was.

He started the engine as instructions came through his earpiece. It was time to capture the last scene for the day's shoot.

The stunt required him to drive the ATV at speed towards the mountain range in the distance. A ramp had been disguised in the dirt and rocks that would flip the vehicle onto its side for dramatic effect. The whole scene could probably be done using CGI techniques and a green screen but the film's director, George Murray, liked as much realism as possible and he had chosen this part of the world for filming because of its authenticity and other-worldliness. It was supposed to be representing another planet and Oliver could see how it could feel that way. He had grown up all around the world but even he'd never seen anywhere that looked as alien and hostile as this.

The setting sun was turning the burnt orange landscape a fiery red. The shadows cast by the distant hills were lengthening and turning violet. He knew the dust thrown up by his tyres would filter the light and lend a sinister aspect to the scene.

He waited for the call of 'action' and pressed his foot to the accelerator. The vehicle leapt forwards. He waited for the tyres to gain traction and then pushed the pedal flat to the floor. The ground was littered with tiny stones, making it difficult to maintain a straight course. He eased off the speed slightly as the vehicle skidded and slid to the left. He corrected the slide without difficulty and continued his course but, just as he thought he'd succeeded, there was a loud bang and the steering wheel shuddered in his hands.

He felt the back of the vehicle slide out to the right and he eased off the speed again as he fought to control it, but the tail had seemingly picked up speed, turning the vehicle ninety degrees to where he wanted it. To where it was supposed to be. He let the wheel spin through his fingers, waiting for the vehicle to straighten, but before he could correct the trajectory the vehicle had gone completely off course. The front tyre dropped into a trough in the dirt and Oliver felt the wheels lift off the ground.

The vehicle began to tip and he knew he had totally lost control. All four wheels were airborne and there was nothing he could do. He couldn't fight it, he couldn't correct it, and he couldn't control it.

The ATV flipped sideways and bounced once. Twice. And again.

It flipped and rolled and Oliver lost count of the cycles as the horizon tumbled before him and the sun's dying rays cast long fingers through the windshield.

Had he finally bitten off more than he could chew?

CHAPTER ONE

OLIVER MASSAGED THE lump on the side of his head. He'd taken a couple of paracetamol for the dull headache but fortunately he'd escaped serious injury yesterday. The bump on his head and some slight bruising on his shoulder were minor complaints and he had no intention of mentioning those aches and pains. The ATV had taken a battering but could be fixed. The repairs meant a change in the filming schedule but nothing that couldn't be accommodated. A serious injury to him would have been far more disruptive.

Despite his luck, however, the incident had made George, the director, wary and Oliver had agreed to hand over some of the stunts to the professionals. The movie couldn't afford for anything to happen to its star and he didn't want to get a reputation as a difficult actor. George had been good to Oliver; he'd worked with him before and he'd been happy to give him another role when other directors had been reluctant, but Oliver knew that being argumentative, disruptive or inflexible wasn't a great way to advance a career. He wasn't stupid, he knew actors were a dime a dozen. He wasn't irreplaceable. No one was. A reputation as a ladies' man was one thing; a reputation as being problematic on set was another thing entirely.

He stretched his neck from side to side as he tried to rid himself of the headache that plagued him. He knew it was from the accident yesterday. He hadn't had that cold beer and had gone to bed alone, so there were no other contributing factors. He knew exactly what had caused his pain.

The schedule change caused by his accident meant he wasn't required for filming this morning, but now he was bored. He wandered around the site, knowing that the heat was probably compounding his headache but too restless to stay indoors.

A whole community had been established temporarily in the middle of the desert just for the movie. Transportable huts were set up as the production centre, the canteen, the first-aid centre, lounge areas for the cast and crew, and Oliver, George and the lead actress all had their own motorhome to retreat to. Marquees surrounded the vehicles and more huts provided additional, and much-needed, shade. The site was twenty miles out of the remote Australian outback town of Coober Pedy, which itself was over three thousand miles from the next major town or, as the Australians said, almost five hundred kilometres. No matter which way you said it, there was no denying that Coober Pedy was a mighty long way from anywhere else.

He'd been completely unprepared for the strangeness of this remote desert town. He'd imagined a flat, barren landscape but the town had sprung up in an area that was far hillier than he'd expected. The main street was tarred and lined with single-level shops and a few taller buildings, including his hotel, with the houses spreading out from the centre of town and into the hills. Along with regular houses there were also hundreds of dwellings dug into the hillsides. He'd heard that people lived underground to escape the merciless heat but he hadn't thought about what that meant in terms of the town's appearance; in effect, it made the town look far more sparsely populated than it actually was.

He knew he should hole up in his trailer and stay out of the heat but he wanted company.

Generators chugged away in the background, providing power for the film set, providing air-conditioning, refrigeration and technology. He was used to having a shower in his trailer but because of water restrictions apparently that was a no-go out here in the Australian desert.

If he moved far enough away from the generators he knew he would hear absolute silence. It should be peaceful, quiet, restful even, and he could understand how some people would find the solitude and the silence soul-restoring, relaxing, but it made him uneasy. He needed more stimulation. He wanted crowds, he wanted noise, he didn't want a chance to be introspective. He was an extrovert, a performer, and as an extrovert he wanted company. He needed company to energise him and as a performer he needed an audience.

He wasn't required on set but he decided he'd go and watch the filming anyway. It would kill some time and give him someone to talk to.

He turned away from the transportable huts that formed the command centre for the movie set and headed towards the vehicle compound. His boots kicked up puffs of red dust as he walked. Everything was coated in dust. It got inside your mouth, your ears, your nostrils. Everything smelt and tasted like dust. It even got inside your eyes—if the flies didn't get there first. Which reminded him that he'd left his sunglasses in his trailer. He spun around; he'd retrieve them and then grab a four-by-four and head further out into the desert to where filming was taking place.

He slipped his glasses on as he stepped back into the heat. Rounding the corner of his trailer, he heard an engine and noticed a dust cloud billowing into the air. He stood in the shade at the corner of his trailer and watched as a car pulled to a stop beside the mess hut. It was an old four-by-four, its brown paintwork covered in red dust, like everything else out here. A haze rose from the bonnet of the car, bringing to mind the story about it being hot enough in Australia to fry an egg in the sun. He believed it.

The car door opened and he waited, his natural curiosity getting the better of him, to see who climbed out.

A woman.

That was unexpected.

She stood and straightened. She was tall, slender, lithe. Her hair was thick and dark and fell just past her shoulders. He watched as she scraped it off her neck and tied it into a loose ponytail, in deference to the heat, he presumed. Her neck was long and swan-like, her limbs long and tanned.

She was stunning and the complete antithesis of what he'd expected, judging from the car she was driving. She reminded him of a butterfly emerging from a cocoon.

He blinked, making sure it wasn't the after-effects of the bump to his head causing his imagination to play tricks on him.

She was still there.

She wore a navy and white summer dress, which must have been lined to mid-thigh, but from there down, with the morning sun behind her, the white sections were completely see-through. He wondered if she knew but he didn't care—her legs were incredible. Magnificent.

Oliver was literally in the middle of nowhere with absolutely nothing of interest to look at. Until now. The middle of nowhere had just become a far more attractive proposition.

He watched as she walked towards him. Graceful. Ethereal. Sunglasses protected her eyes but her skin was flawless and her lips were full and painted with bright red lipstick. The shade was striking against her olive skin and raven hair.

He'd seen plenty of beautiful woman in his thirty-two years, he was surrounded by them on a daily basis, but he didn't think he'd ever seen a woman as naturally beautiful. The ones he worked with had all had some help—a scalpel here, an injection there—and he'd swear on his father's grave, something he hoped he would be able to do sooner rather than later, that she hadn't had any assistance.

He watched, not moving a muscle, scared that any movement might startle her, might make her shimmer and disappear, mirage-like, into the desert.

Maybe his headache was affecting his thought processes; maybe he'd been out in the sun for too long, or simply in the outback for too long. Other than the cast and crew he'd barely seen another person for days. The hot, dusty streets of Coober Pedy were, for the most part, empty. The locals hunkered down in their underground dwellings to escape the heat, venturing out only briefly and if absolutely necessary, scampering from one building to the subterranean comfort of the next. But perhaps many of the locals looked like this. Perhaps that was the attraction in this desolate, baked and barren desert town.

She had stopped walking as her gaze scanned the buildings, looking for something or someone. Looking lost. His curiosity was piqued. His attention captured.

Her gaze landed on him and she took another step forward. Belatedly he stepped out of the shadows and walked towards her; he'd been so transfixed he'd forgotten to move, forgotten his manners, but he wanted to be the first to offer her assistance.

'Hello, I'm Oliver; may I help you?'

She stopped and waited as he approached her.

'Thank you,' she said. 'I'm looking for George Murray.' Her voice was deep and slightly breathless, without the broad Australian accent that he'd heard so many of the crew speak with. She glanced down at her watch and his eyes followed. Her watch had a large face, with the numbers clearly marked and an obvious hand counting off the seconds. Her fingers were delicate by comparison, long and slender, with short nails lacquered with clear varnish. He was trained to be observant, to watch people's mannerisms, to listen to their voices, but even so he was aware that he was soaking up everything about this woman. From the colour of her lips and the shine of her hair, to the smooth lustre of her skin and the inflection of her speech. He wanted to be able to picture her perfectly later. She lifted her head. 'I have an interview with him at eleven.'

'A job interview?'

She nodded. 'Of sorts.'

'Are you going to be working on the film? Are you an extra?'

'No.'

'Catering? Publicity?'

'No and no.' Her mouth turned up at one corner and he got a glimpse of perfect, even white teeth bordered by those red lips.

He grinned. 'You're not going to tell me?'

Her smile widened and he knew she was enjoying the repartee. 'No, I don't think I am.'

Two could play at that game. 'All right, then,' he shrugged, feigning disinterest, 'George is out on set but he shouldn't be long. Filming started early today to try to beat the heat, so they'll be breaking for lunch soon. Let me show you to his trailer.' He'd take her to where she needed to go but he wouldn't leave her.

He bounced lightly up the two steps that led to George's office and pushed open the heavy metal door. He flicked on the lights and held the door for her. She brushed past him and her breasts lightly grazed his arm but she showed no sign that she'd noticed the contact. She stopped just inside the door and removed her sunglasses, and he caught a trace of her scent—fresh, light and fruity.

He watched as she surveyed the interior. An enormous television screen dominated the wall opposite the desk, which was covered in papers. A laptop sat open amongst the mess. A large fridge with a glass door was tucked into a corner to the left, and a couch was pressed against the opposite wall with two armchairs at right angles to it and a small coffee table in between.

He wondered if this was what she'd expected to see.

'Have a seat,' he invited as he waved an arm towards the chairs. She sat but avoided the couch.

'Can I get you something to drink?'

She nodded and the light bounced off her hair, making it look like silk. 'A water would be lovely, thank you.'

He grabbed a glass and two bottles of mineral water from the fridge. He twisted the tops off and passed her the glass and a bottle.

'I'll be fine waiting here,' she said as she took the drink from him. 'You must have something you need to do?'

He shook his head as he sat on the couch. He leant back and rested one foot on his other knee, relaxed, comfortable, approachable, conveying candidness. 'I'm not busy. The scene they're filming doesn't involve me.'

'You're an actor?'

He looked carefully at her to gauge if she was joking but her expression was serious. Her mouth looked serious, her red lips full but not moving. But was there a hint of humour in her dark eyes? He couldn't read her yet. Perhaps she was an anomaly, someone who didn't immediately recognise him, or maybe he just wasn't famous out here in the middle of nowhere.

Should he tell her who he was?

No. That could wait. She still hadn't told him what she was doing here. She'd said she wasn't publicity but she could be a journalist. He didn't need more reporters telling stories about him. But if that was the case, surely she would recognise him.

Unless she was a better actor than he was, he was certain she wasn't a reporter.

He settled for vague. 'I am,' he said as the door opened again and George entered the trailer.

'Kat! Welcome.' He was beaming. Oliver was surprised; George never looked this pleased to see anyone. George was a little rotund, always in a hurry, and seemed to have a permanent scowl creasing his forehead. Seeing him so delighted to see another person was somewhat disconcerting.

He crossed the room as the woman stood. Kat or Kate, Oliver thought George had said, but he wasn't quite sure. Oliver stood too; manners that had been instilled in him, growing up as the son of a strict military man, remained automatic.

George greeted her with a kiss and Oliver was more intrigued. There was obviously some history here that he wasn't privy to. Who was she?

'I see you've met our star, Oliver Harding.'

'Not formally.' She turned to him and extended her hand. 'I'm Katarina Angelis, but call me Kat.' Her handshake was firm but it was the softness of her skin and the laughter in her eyes that caught Oliver off guard. 'It's a pleasure to meet you.'

He realised she'd known exactly who he was. Which put him at a disadvantage. He still knew nothing about her. But he did know her name seemed to suit her perfectly. He was sure Katarina meant 'pure', and Angelis had to mean 'heavenly'.

'The pleasure is all mine,' he said.

George cleared his throat and Oliver realised he hadn't let go of Kat's hand. He also realised he didn't want to. Beautiful women were everywhere in his world, but there was something more to Kat. Something intriguing. Something different.

Her skin was soft and cool. Flawless. She looked like a desert rose, a surprising beauty in the harshness of the outback, and he found himself transfixed by her scarlet mouth. Her lips brought to mind ripe summer cherries, dark red and juicy. He wondered how they'd taste.

'If I might give you some advice, my dear,' George said to Kat as Oliver finally let her hand drop, 'you should stay away from Oliver.'

'Hey!' he protested.

'You don't have to worry about me, George,' Kat replied. 'I can handle myself.'

George shook his head. 'You've never met anyone like Oliver.'

Kat was looking at him now. Studying him, as if sizing him up and comparing him to George's assessment. Oliver smiled and shrugged and spread his hands wide, proclaiming his innocence. He had to take it on the chin; he couldn't remonstrate with George in front of Kat—it would be better to laugh it off. He couldn't afford to show how she'd affected him. It was safer to return to his usual persona of charm and confidence, of not taking himself or anyone too seriously. She had floored him and he needed to gather his wits and work out what to do about it. About her. But, for now, he'd play along. 'George is right, Kat, I'm the man your father warned you about.'

She laughed. 'Don't go thinking that makes you special. My father is always warning me about men.'

He cocked his head and quirked one eyebrow. This was even better. He had never been one to back away from a challenge.

'Don't make me regret hiring you.' George eyeballed them both. 'Either of you.'

Oliver laughed; he was used to being told off, but he was surprised to see that Kat was blushing. She looked even more delightful now.

'I mean it, Oliver—don't mess with Kat.' George looked him straight in the eye. 'There aren't too many places left for you to run to and if you hurt her you'll want to start running, believe me.'

So now they were both going to put a challenge to him. Of course, that only served to entice him even more. George could warn him all he liked but Oliver had never been one to steer clear of a challenge. But he knew he had to tread carefully. He couldn't afford any more scandals.

'Go and find something to do,' George told him. 'I need to talk to Kat.'

Oliver left but he knew it wouldn't be the last he saw of Kat Angelis. He was glad now that she hadn't admitted that she recognised him, that she hadn't said his reputation preceded him. Perhaps she'd have no preconceived ideas about him and he could try to impress her without any rumours or innuendo getting in the way.

He was still none the wiser as to her actual reason for being on set but, if George was hiring her, he'd make sure their paths crossed again. If he was going to be stuck in this town for the next few weeks he might as well have some fun. He knew it was his choice, almost, to be here—George had made him an offer that his publicist thought was too good to refuse—and timing was everything. But that didn't mean he couldn't enjoy himself. He wouldn't misbehave, but even if he did he doubted anyone would ever hear about what went on out here. Coober Pedy and the Australian outback seemed to exist in its own little time capsule. It really was a whole other world.

Kat watched on as George shooed Oliver out of his office. Of course she'd recognised him—Oliver Harding was a star of multiple

Hollywood blockbusters. He had been the lead actor in several recent box office hits and he played action heroes just as well as he carried romantic leads. He was in the news regularly, if not for his movies then for his off-screen exploits with his leading ladies or other Hollywood 'It' girls. Kat may be a small-town girl, living out in the desert in the middle of nowhere, but she had television, magazines, the internet and the local drive-in movie theatre, which showed new movies every Saturday night. Oliver Harding was famous and she would have to be living under a rock not to know who he was. The thought made her smile. She did actually live underground, like so many of the local residents, but that didn't mean she didn't know what went on in the rest of the world. Oliver Harding appeared in a new movie every six months, and with a new woman far more frequently. Having met him now, she could understand why. He was handsome on the silver screen but incredibly gorgeous in real life. He had charm, charisma and a twinkle in his bright blue eyes that had made her lose her train of thought on more than one occasion already.

'I'm serious, Kat,' George cautioned her again. Had he mistaken her smile to mean she wasn't paying attention to his warning?

'I've seen that look in his eye before. You really don't want him to set his sights on you. Stronger women than you have fallen for his charms. He loves the thrill of the chase and he hates to let a pretty girl go unappreciated, but he has a tendency to leave a trail of broken hearts behind him.'

He had a cheeky appeal and amazing eyes and his smile made her stomach tumble, but Kat wasn't about to succumb to his charm. She'd met charming men before and didn't intend to be another notch on his bedpost. And she hadn't been kidding when she'd said she knew how to handle herself. There was no denying Oliver Harding was gorgeous and charming but she was *not* the type to fall for charming and handsome. Well, that wasn't technically true but she wasn't the type to have flings with famous men who were just visiting. That was something irresponsible people did. Spontaneous people. And she'd learnt not to be either of those.

'Don't worry about me, George. I really can handle myself.'

'He has a reputation for seducing women, but, in his defence, don't believe everything you read or hear. He's a nice guy but still a flirt and definitely incorrigible.'

'I'm here to work, not fool around with

the staff,' Kat stated, reminding herself of her obligations as much as she was reminding George. 'So, what exactly did you want to see me about?'

George sighed. 'Oliver has it written into his contract that he gets to do a proportion of his own stunt work. A large proportion. But yesterday things didn't go quite to plan. He was involved in an accident. The vehicle he was driving was supposed to crash but instead of going into a controlled sideways tip it flipped at speed and ended up on its roof. He seems to be fine.'

Kat thought back—she hadn't noticed a limp or any bruising or protective postures, but she hadn't been looking for signs of injury. She'd been too focused on his mesmerising blue eyes and on trying not to act like a star-struck fan.

'But,' George continued, 'since the incident our first-aid officer is refusing to be responsible for Oliver's safety and I must say she has a point. We have a stunt coordinator who is also Oliver's double but…sometimes things go wrong. I think it would be prudent to have someone on set who has more experience than just a first-aid qualification. Not full-time, just when we're doing the stunts. Do you think, if I gave you the filming schedule, you might be able to work with us? Would you be interested?'

'I think so.' George had outlined his thoughts on the phone to her last night but she needed more details. 'Can you give me a basic idea of what would be required, mainly how much time?'

She listened as George ran through the filming schedule with her.

'I'd still need to be available for ambulance shifts—even with the volunteers we don't have enough staff to allow me to give those up,' Kat said. Getting qualified paramedics to work in rural and remote areas was always tough and Kat knew she would have to make sure she didn't put her colleagues under any additional pressure by requesting time off in order to do something that was purely to satisfy her own desires. As tempting and exciting as it was to think of working on a movie set, not to mention with Oliver Harding, her commitment to her career had to be her priority.

'We could work around your schedule to a certain degree. As long as you could be on set when we're doing the stunt work. Would that be possible? I don't want to wear you out.'

From what George had described to her last night, the movie wasn't really her cup of tea— she preferred drama and thrillers to science fiction—but she had to admit it would be exciting to work on a film set, and getting to work with Oliver would be an added bonus.

'I reckon I can work something out. I'll see if I can swap some of my day shifts for nights. We're on call overnight. With a resident population of just over two thousand people there's not usually a lot to keep us busy. It's tourists that swell our numbers and keep us occupied.'

'That's great. I'll get a contract drawn up; you'll be fairly paid for your time.'

'I don't need—'

'Don't argue,' George interrupted. 'I need it to be all above board and your wages will be a drop in the ocean that is our budget. Think of it as spending money—put it aside and treat yourself to something.'

Kat couldn't remember the last time she'd treated herself to something. She couldn't even begin to imagine what she would do, but it was easier to agree.

'There is one other thing,' George added. 'A favour. I need some extra locations. The cave where I wanted to shoot is apparently sacred Aboriginal land and I can't get permission to film there. You don't happen to know of anything else around here?'

'I do know something that might do,' Kat replied. 'It's on my godfather's land about ten minutes out of town. I can take you out to see it later today if you like. Shall I meet you at the hotel?'

Kat picked up the copy of the film schedule that George had given her, kissed him goodbye and made arrangements to meet at five. She stepped out of the trailer and found Oliver waiting for her.

'Now are you going to tell me what you're doing here?' he asked as he fell into step beside her. His voice was deep and pleasant, his accent neutral. She'd expected more of an American flavour. Had he been taught to tone it down?

'I live here.'

'Really? Here?'

She could hear the unspoken question, the one every visitor asked until they got to know Coober Pedy. *Why?*

She never knew where to start. How did one begin to explain the beauty, the peace, the wildness, the attraction? She loved it here. That didn't mean she never entertained the idea of travelling the world and seeing other places, but this was home. This was where her family lived. And family was everything.

She had no idea how to explain all of that, so she simply said, 'Yes, really.'

'But you know George?' He was walking

closely beside her and his arm brushed against hers every few steps, interrupting her concentration.

She nodded.

'Are you going to tell me how?'

'It's not my story to tell.'

'At least tell me why you have the filming schedule, then.'

She stopped walking and turned to look at him. She had to look up. She wasn't short—she was five feet nine inches tall—but still he was several inches taller. 'Are you always this nosy?'

'Yes.' He was smiling. 'Although I prefer to think of myself as having an enquiring mind. It sounds more masculine. I'm happy to be in touch with my feminine side, but only in private.'

'I'm going to be working on the film,' she said, hoping to surprise him.

'Doing what?'

'Keeping *you* out of trouble,' she said as she continued towards her car.

'Trouble is my middle name,' he laughed.

She didn't doubt that. She'd only known him for a few minutes and regardless of George's warning she already had the sense that he was trouble. But she couldn't help smiling as she said, 'So I hear.'

Kat reached her car and stretched her hand out to open the door, which she hadn't bothered locking, but Oliver was faster than she was. He rested his hand on the door frame, preventing her from opening it.

'And just how exactly do you plan to keep me out of trouble?' His voice was deep and sexy, perfect for a leading man.

She turned to face him. He was standing close. Her eyes were level with his chest. He was solid—muscular without being beefy, gym-toned. He didn't look as if he'd done a hard day's work in his life, and he probably hadn't, but that didn't stop him from being handsome. With his chiselled good looks, he could have come straight from the pages of a men's fashion magazine.

He smelt good. He looked even better.

His blue eyes were piercing, his square jaw clean-shaven. His thick brown hair was cut in a short back and sides, slightly longer on top, like a military-style haircut that had been on holiday for a couple of weeks. She wondered if it was to fit the movie script or if it was how he chose to cut his hair. It suited him. It emphasised his bone structure.

'I'm your insurance policy,' she said.

He frowned and raised one eyebrow. She wondered if that came naturally or if he'd cultivated that move. Was it possible to learn how to do that?

'I'm a paramedic,' she continued. 'I'm going to be on set for the stunt work. Just in case.'

She'd expected him to object but he took it in his stride.

'Good,' he said simply before he grinned widely. 'I'll be seeing plenty of you, then.'

He was so confident, so comfortable. She wondered if he'd ever been told he couldn't do something. She imagined that if he had he would have chosen to ignore the instruction.

His arm was still outstretched, passing beside her head as he leant against her car. 'So, Kat, tell me your story.'

'Why do you want to know?'

She was caught between his chest and the car. She could step out, away from the boundaries he'd imposed, but she didn't want to. She didn't feel threatened. He was smiling at her. He looked genuine, friendly, but she needed to remember he was an actor. He was probably trained to smile in a hundred different ways. She remembered George's warning but she chose to ignore it. Just for a moment. She wanted to see what would happen next. She felt as if she was in a movie moment of her own.

His smile widened, showcasing teeth that

were white, even and perfect. His blue eyes sparkled. 'Because I want to make sure I'm not overstepping any lines when I ask you out.'

He looked like a man who was used to getting his own way and she didn't doubt that; with women, at least, he probably did. But she did doubt that she was the type of woman he was used to meeting. 'And what makes you think I'd go out with you?'

'I didn't say you would, I'm just letting you know I will ask you to. The choice is completely yours.'

'What did you have in mind?' She shouldn't ask but she wanted to know. She should heed George's warning and get in her car and drive away but it had been a long time since she'd been asked on a date and she was interested to hear his thoughts. She was interested full stop.

He smiled. 'I don't know yet but I'll think of something.'

There weren't a lot of options in Coober Pedy and Oliver, not being a local, would know even fewer.

Kat couldn't remember the last time someone had flirted with her or the last time she'd met anyone she wanted to flirt with. She couldn't deny she was flattered by the attention. She'd need to be careful. She'd been hurt before; a monumental break-up had left her questioning her own judgement and she'd avoided getting romantically involved ever since. She wanted her own happily-ever-after but she'd been scared to go out to find it. She'd focused instead on her career and her family and it had been a while since she'd even thought about going on a date. George's warning repeated in her head again but she had no idea if she was going to be able to heed it.

The touch of Oliver's hand had set her pulse racing and the look in his eye had made her wish, just momentarily, that she was the sort of girl who would take a risk, take a chance.

But that wasn't her. She'd learnt that taking risks was asking for trouble, and Oliver Harding had trouble written all over him.

CHAPTER TWO

KAT PULLED INTO the courtyard in front of the Cave Hotel. She found a spot to park under a gum tree in the shadow of the hill, seeking shade out of habit rather than necessity at this time of the evening. The air was still warm but the searing heat of the day was beginning to dissipate.

The sun was setting behind the hotel, turning the sky orange. The hotel was the town's only five-star accommodation. Kat doubted it could be compared to five-star indulgence in Paris, London or New York but it was luxurious by Coober Pedy standards and all that Kat knew. She'd never travelled outside Australia and had never stayed in anything rated above three and a half stars.

'Do you have a little more time up your sleeve?' George asked as Kat switched off her car. 'As a thank-you for showing me those caves I'll buy you a cold drink and introduce you to the cast. I imagine they'll gather in the bar before dinner and it would be a good chance to meet them before you start work.'

'Sure,' she replied. 'I'll just make a call and then I'll meet you inside.'

Like a lot of the dwellings in town, the hotel had been built into the side of a hill. It had newer wings that extended out from the hill but Kat always recommended that people book an underground room as a preference, for the atmosphere and experience plus the fact that the rooms were bigger and cooler. The original, subterranean floorplan had been designed to enable the rooms to maintain a constant temperature year-round, a bonus in the scorching heat of summer and during cold winter nights, but it meant that cell phone reception could be erratic inside.

The hotel had air-conditioning, an excellent restaurant and shops, and the courtyard parking area had been covered in bitumen, which, in contrast to the dusty streets, was perhaps all that was needed. More importantly it had an outdoor pool, secluded behind an adobe wall and surrounded by palm trees. Kat had always thought the palms a bit incongruous, considering the environment, but they seemed to thrive.

She stepped under the covered walkway that

ran from the pool to the hotel foyer, seeking
the shade. She called her father, letting him
know she'd be late and checking that he was
happy to wait for dinner. As she finished her
phone call she heard the pool gate slam shut
behind her. She turned her head and saw Oliver walking her way.

He had a beach towel slung over his right
shoulder but he was still wet. He was bare-
chested, his skin smooth and slick and golden
brown. Damp swimming trunks hugged his
thighs.

Kat's mouth went dry as she tried not to
ogle him, but it was a difficult task. Eventually she lifted her eyes and saw him smiling at
her. His smile was incredible. It started slowly;
one corner of his mouth lifted first and then
his smile stretched across his lips before they
parted to reveal perfect white teeth and a wide,
engaging smile.

'This is a pleasant surprise. I didn't expect
to see you. What are you up to?'

He stopped at her side, took the towel from
his shoulder and started to dry his chest. There
was a purple bruise on his right shoulder and
Kat was going to ask about it, but that was before she got distracted. Oliver's arm muscles
flexed as he rubbed the towel over his body,
diverting her attention. He ran the towel over

his abdomen and she couldn't help but follow his movements. His stomach muscles rippled as he twisted to reach his hand behind his back and Kat's heart skipped a beat as she forced herself to concentrate. She was yearning to reach out and run her hand over his shoulder and down his arm. To feel his biceps tense and flex under her fingers. If she thought he was attractive fully clothed then he was something else altogether when he was partially naked.

She swallowed as she tried to rein in her imagination. 'I've just brought George back—we went to scout some locations.'

'You've already got the lingo, I see,' he said as he slung the towel back over his shoulder. 'What are you doing now?'

'I'm having a drink at the bar. George is going to introduce me to a few people.'

'Great, I'll see you inside.' He started walking towards the hotel and Kat focused on walking beside him, on putting one foot in front of the other.

He held the lobby door open for her but stopped at the entrance to the bar. 'I'm not dressed appropriately—I'll get changed and come back. Are you OK to go in by yourself?'

Kat wasn't used to people checking on her; everyone in town knew her and the locals expected people to look after themselves. On

the whole women weren't treated any differently to men but she stopped herself from giving a short reply of 'of course', as she realised
he was just being polite. He was just treating
her with courtesy, showing some respect. It
was something her father would have done
for her mother.

Her father would have been horrified if
her mother had gone into a hotel unaccompanied. When they had been courting there
would have been separate bars for the men and
women, and women would never have been
permitted in the 'public' bar, but times had
changed and no one now would bat an eye-
lid at a woman going into a bar alone. Kat
knew she would feel uncomfortable in a different setting, in a different town, but everyone
knew her here; she still appreciated Oliver's
manners though. She nodded. 'Yes, I'm fine,
thank you.'

The bar was cool and softly lit. It was in the
original part of the hotel, dug into the hill. Its
walls and ceilings were the colour of ochre,
the same colour as the land, but the walls had
been coated with a clear lacquer to stop the
dust that would otherwise coat everything in
its path. It was a large room and felt spacious
even though there were no windows. Indoor
plants helped to delineate the space, creating

smaller areas and a sense of privacy while helping to disguise the fact that they were several feet under the surface.

George was waiting for her and introduced her to several of the cast and crew as she nursed the drink he had purchased for her. She tried to focus on who everyone was but she was constantly scanning the room, waiting for Oliver to return. She hated knowing that she was waiting for him, looking forward to seeing him, but she couldn't help the feeling.

She did a slight double-take when a tall man walked in—his build and even his gait were so similar to Oliver's that it wasn't until he removed his cap that she registered that not only was he not Oliver, but he also had a shaved head and was not nearly as good-looking. But his movements had been similar enough that she'd had to look twice, so it was no surprise when George introduced him as Chris, the man who was Oliver's stunt double. Kat shook his hand, noticing his brown eyes even as she noted that the touch of his hand didn't set her heart racing. He was pleasant enough, fit and young, but very definitely not Oliver.

'When you see Oliver,' Chris said to George after shaking Kat's hand, 'let him know I'll meet him in the gym for his training session.'

He turned to Kat. 'Good to meet you, Kat; I'll see you on set.'

When Oliver finally entered the bar, Kat wondered how she could have mistaken Chris for him. There was an aura about Oliver, something drew her to him and she found it almost impossible to turn away.

'Hello, Kat.' He was looking at her intensely. Did he look at everyone like that? she wondered.

She felt as though he could see inside her, see all her secrets. Not that she had any. Something about him made her wish she was a little mysterious, wish she wasn't so ordinary. She wished there was something about her that could intrigue him.

'Chris is waiting in the gym for you.' George was speaking to Oliver and his voice brought her back to the present.

'That's OK, I promised Kat a drink first. Chris will wait.'

Kat opened her mouth to object—Oliver hadn't promised her any such thing—but before she could speak he winked at her and grinned and she kept quiet.

George's assistant, Erica, came to the table and spoke softly in George's ear.

'If you'll excuse me, I need to speak to Julia.

It appears she is having a crisis.' George stood before adding, 'Behave yourself, Oliver.'

Oliver just grinned in reply, apparently brushing George's warning aside without a thought as George left the table, leaving them alone and leaving Kat a little nervous. To fill in the pause in conversation she asked, 'Will she be OK?'

'Have you met our leading lady yet?' Oliver replied.

Kat shook her head.

'Julia is always in the middle of a crisis,' Oliver told her. 'I attract scandals, she attracts crises. We probably shouldn't be allowed to work together. There's always a danger of too much drama.' He laughed and Kat found herself relaxing. 'Now, tell me, what are you drinking?' he said.

'Are you sure you shouldn't be meeting Chris?'

Oliver shrugged and shook his head. 'Not yet.'

'Won't you be in trouble?'

'I'm used to it. Trust me, you are far better company than Chris, not to mention better-looking, and I might not get this opportunity again.' He smiled his slow, drawn-out smile and Kat's stomach flipped and fluttered in response. It was almost as though his smile kept time with his thoughts but she felt at a distinct disadvantage because, while she could hazard a guess, she actually had no idea what his thoughts were.

'Besides, I told you trouble is my middle name.'

Kat smiled back. There was no denying his charm. 'Maybe trouble should have been your first name.'

Oliver laughed as he stood up and even his laugh was perfect. Deep and rich, he sounded like someone who laughed often. 'Chris will make me sweat for making him wait. I might as well enjoy a beer if he's going to take his revenge in dead lifts and push-ups anyway.'

'OK, thank you; a beer sounds good,' Kat said, accepting his invitation.

'Explain to me how the stunt double thing works,' she said when Oliver returned from the bar. 'I get that Chris has a similar physique to you and even moves a bit the same, but he doesn't look like you. Is that a problem? Is that why you're doing some of your own stunts?'

'No. Chris has been my body double on several movies and he wears a wig if needed, but in this movie he's often wearing a helmet, so his hair, or lack of it, is irrelevant.'

'What about his eyes?' Oliver's were such a

distinctive, vibrant blue, Kat couldn't see how they could work around that.

'He's not in any close-up shots, so we don't need to see his eyes, but he could probably wear coloured contact lenses if necessary. The make-up girls are good and nowadays there's always CGI.'

Oliver was distracted by something over Kat's right shoulder. She wondered if Chris had come to force him into the gym and so was surprised when she heard her name.

'Kat?'

She turned to find her cousin, Dean, and his wife, Saskia, standing behind her. While she knew almost everyone in town, she hadn't been expecting to see any familiar faces in this particular bar. The Cave Hotel was expensive and usually frequented exclusively by tourists.

Kat stood up and greeted them both with a kiss. 'Hi. What are you doing here?'

'Dean is taking me to dinner at Mona's. It's our wedding anniversary.'

The hotel restaurant, Mona's, was the best in town and was the one drawcard for the locals, who often chose to dine there to celebrate special occasions.

'Of course it is,' Kat replied. 'Happy anniversary.' But Saskia had turned her attention to Oliver by now and was looking at him with interest.

'Hello. I'm Saskia and this is my husband, Dean.'

Oliver was already on his feet. 'Oliver Harding,' he said as he shook Saskia's hand and then Dean's.

'What are you two up to?' Dean asked.

Kat could see the look of approval on Saskia's face but, whereas her expression was one of appreciation, Dean looked wary. That wasn't unexpected—Kat, Dean and his brother, Roger, were more like siblings than cousins and the boys had always been protective of Kat, particularly when it came to who she dated, but she didn't need Dean trying to rescue her from this situation. There wasn't a situation at all. This was just a work meeting.

To his credit Oliver didn't seem fazed by Dean's abrupt question but Kat jumped in before Oliver could say anything that could be misconstrued. She didn't need any rumours getting back to her father. 'Oliver is an actor in the movie that's being shot in town. I'm going to be working with him.'

'As what?' Dean asked. His piercing gaze would have pinned a lesser man to the spot but Oliver seemed completely unperturbed by the attention.

'The emergency response officer,' Kat replied.

'That sounds appealing,' Saskia said with a slight smirk. Kat glared at her but Saskia just smiled, while Dean continued to size Oliver up.

Kat watched them both. Oliver was squaring up to Dean and she wondered if she'd need to step in between them. As fit as Oliver was, she wasn't sure he'd be a match for her cousin in a physical confrontation.

The men were much the same height, both a couple of inches over six feet, but Dean was probably twenty kilograms heavier with a hardness about him that Kat knew came from growing up in this environment. Oliver's muscles came from gym work, which was different from the muscles gained from working outdoors in the heat and dust of the Australian outback. Dean was neat and tidy but he had a toughness about him, except when he was with his wife and kids.

Oliver was groomed, not tough, still all male but a more polished version. He was gorgeous but, as far as Kat knew, he was used to Hollywood. In comparison, Dean was used to the outback, which was tough and rugged and, Kat imagined, just about as far from Hollywood as it was possible to get. Dean's life couldn't be more different from Oliver's.

'And what exactly does that entail?' Dean asked.

'It's exciting. I'll tell you about it over dinner,' Saskia said as she tucked her arm into Dean's elbow and prepared to lead him through the bar and into the restaurant.

Kat had told Saskia about the job offer. Saskia and Dean had been together since high school and Saskia was like a sister to Kat. As an only child, she appreciated the relationship she had with her cousin's wife. She was slightly envious of her cousins' marriages; they had what she wished for. They had found their 'one'.

Once upon a time, Kat had had that too. She had thought she was going to get her own happily-ever-after, but things hadn't turned out how she'd expected and now she was starting to wonder if she was ever going to find her soulmate. She was pretty sure she wasn't going to find him in Coober Pedy—the town was dwindling; people were leaving. Would she have to leave too?

'I would jump at the chance to take on that job if I didn't have you and the kids and work to worry about,' Saskia said, bringing Kat back to the present, 'if I was single and free, like Kat,' she added, directing her less than subtle remark to Oliver.

Kat needed to move them on before Saskia said something that would embarrass her. She hugged them both and said, 'Enjoy your dinner,' as she put some gentle pressure against the small of Saskia's back, encouraging her to leave and take Dean with her.

But Saskia wasn't done yet. 'Will we see you on Sunday or are you working?'

'I'll be there.'

'What's happening on Sunday?' Oliver asked when they were alone again.

'Family dinner.' It was a weekly occurrence and there was an expectation that everyone would attend, but Kat didn't mind. She adored her family. Kat had moved back in with her father after her mother passed away, and her extended family—her aunt Rosa, Dean and Saskia, Roger and his wife, Maya, and their children—had dinner together every Sunday.

'Family?'

Kat nodded. 'Dean is my cousin.'

'Your cousin! Do you have other family here?'

'Yes, of course. My whole family is here. This is where I grew up.'

'Here?'

'Yes. I told you that.'

'No. You never said you grew up here. You told me you lived here. Those are two different things.'

'I know what you're thinking,' Kat said.

'How can you know what I'm thinking?'

'Because it's what everyone who's not from here thinks. You assumed I moved here for work because why would someone *choose* to live here?'

'I guess I did think it was for your job,' Oliver agreed. 'But that's partly because everyone I know moves where their job takes them.'

'I've lived here my entire life, just about.' Give or take a few years in Adelaide, but she tried not to think too much about those years. 'I choose to live here because my family is here. And because I miss it when I'm not here.'

'What do you miss?'

'The community. The people. The beauty.' She could see from his expression that he didn't believe her. 'I'll show you. There's more to the outback than dust and flies.'

'It's a date,' Oliver said, smiling again, and Kat realised, just a fraction too late, that he'd played her and got just what he wanted.

'It's not a date,' she protested.

'You can call it whatever you like,' he said with a smile, 'but I'm going to call it a date.'

He reached towards her and Kat thought

he was going to pick up her empty glass, but his fingers reached for her hand. His thumb stroked the side of her wrist before he turned her hand over and ran his thumb over the sensitive skin on the underside. Kat's insides turned liquid, she felt as though her bones were melting, and it took all her energy not to close her eyes and give in to the heat that flooded through her.

She needed to leave. To get out from under the spell he was casting over her. She was feeling vulnerable and she knew she was in danger of falling for his charm. He created an energy around him, around her.

'I should go,' she said as she pulled her hand away, breaking the spell before she made a complete fool of herself.

'I guess I'd better get to the gym,' he said as he stood, 'but I'll walk you to your car first.'

He kept a slight distance between them as they walked outside but even so she was aware of a field of attraction and desire surrounding them. Or at least surrounding her.

She turned towards him as they stopped at her car.

'I'll see you at work,' he said as he opened the door that she'd once again left unlocked. 'And I'm looking forward to our date,' he added, 'but until then…' he said as he bent his head and leant towards her.

Kat didn't intend to but she lifted her face, angling it up to him.

Was he going to kiss her?

Her eyelids drifted down, half-closed.

She could feel his breath on her cheek and then his lips pressed against her cheek, just in front of her ear, briefly touching her. Too briefly.

She opened her eyes.

He'd kissed her but not how she'd expected him to. Not how she wanted him to.

He was watching her and she knew he could read her mind. She'd wanted him to kiss her properly. She knew it and he knew it.

She needed to get a grip, she thought as she slid into her car. She was sure he had the same effect on dozens, hundreds, of women. Just because she felt something didn't mean he did. He probably didn't notice it. It was probably something he did out of habit. George had warned her but she couldn't ignore or deny the feelings he evoked in her. She shouldn't be so fascinated but she hadn't met anyone like him. Ever. It was as if he was from a different world.

He scared her. Not in a frightening sense but in a sense that he would have seen far more than she ever had; she had no doubt he would have had his share of beautiful women around the world and she wasn't worldly enough to compete. She didn't *want* to compete. Not unless she knew she could win. And she suspected there would only be one winner if she let Oliver Harding get his way.

She was certain he was not the man for her. Just as she knew she wasn't the woman for him. She wasn't going to be anyone's conquest. But she couldn't deny he was attractive. Charming. And sexy.

She knew it would be almost impossible to deny her desire if he kept up his charm offensive, so she suspected the question wasn't *could* she resist him, but rather how long could she resist him for?

'Good morning! How was your date?'

Kat jumped, spilling her coffee over the kitchen bench as Saskia's voice interrupted her morning routine. 'Jesus, Sas, you scared the life out of me.'

'Daydreaming about a cute actor, were you?'

'No,' Kat fibbed. 'And it wasn't a date.'

'Looked like one to me.'

'I was just there to meet some of the cast and crew,' she said as she mopped up the spilt coffee. But she couldn't help the blush she could feel creeping across her cheeks as Saskia's comment reminded her that she had promised Oliver a date. At least, in his words she had.

Saskia raised one eyebrow but didn't comment. She leant on the kitchen bench and sipped from her own mug that she'd brought in with her. Kat knew it would still be hot; Saskia hadn't come far. She and Dean lived next door.

Saskia and Dean, Roger and Maya, plus Kat's aunt and uncle all lived in the same street, with their underground houses dug into the same hill. As their family had expanded they had simply dug more rooms and added new entrances so they all had their own front door. Kat's own parents had dug a house in the same hill and she had moved back in with her father when she returned to Coober Pedy from Adelaide. She didn't mind living close to her family—she enjoyed the feeling of belonging—but sometimes the proximity could be disconcerting.

If the houses were viewed from outside, all that was obvious were the front doors and some windows. Gardens, or what passed for gardens in the arid country, were at the front, complete with barbecues or pizza ovens and outdoor seating areas used on the warm nights. The houses themselves extended back into the hill. Internally her father's house had white, lime-washed walls, which gave a welcome break from the perpetual sight of red earth. A few skylights and air vents protruded from the surface, but there was no way of telling how large the houses were from outside, and some were very large.

'When do you start work on the movie?' Saskia asked as she sat down at the kitchen table.

'I'm going out to the set this morning, but only to get a feel for filming. There are no stunts today.'

Saskia looked Kat up and down. 'Is that what you're wearing?'

Kat was wearing black three-quarter-length trousers and a loose camisole top. The clothes were comfortable and cool, perfect for the late autumn heatwave they were experiencing, but she could tell by Saskia's tone that she didn't approve. 'What's wrong with this?'

'Nothing, if you don't mind Oliver seeing you dressed like a homeless person.'

'I'm not dressing for him,' she said, even as she began to rethink her outfit.

'You're right. It probably doesn't matter. He probably doesn't care what you're wearing—he's only interested in getting you out of your clothes.'

'Saskia!'

'How about you?' Saskia continued, ignoring Kat's exclamation. 'Are you interested? You'd have to be comatose not to be.'

'He's not my type.'

'What? Drop-dead gorgeous isn't your type?'

Kat smiled but shook her head at the same time. 'He could have his pick of women—what would he want with a country girl like me? Even if he did set his sights on me, I'm not going to fall for him just because his pickings are limited out here.' How did she explain to Saskia that he made her nervous and that it was a mixture of excitement and uncertainty? She suspected he was far too experienced for her, and she didn't want Saskia to laugh at her by telling her so.

'I'm pretty sure he's already set his sights on you, and it wouldn't matter where you were, Kat, you'd get noticed. But if you think you can't handle him…' Saskia paused, waiting for a response, but when nothing was forthcoming she continued '…then you might as well go dressed as you are, or I could find you something else to wear?'

* * *

Kat checked her make-up in her rear vision mirror. She wasn't wearing much as it was too hot and most of it would just slide off her face, but she touched up her signature red lipstick, telling herself she didn't want to look like a country cousin in comparison to the actors on set but not admitting that she was really driven by a desire to look good for Oliver. She felt a little silly that she'd let Saskia talk her into changing her outfit but she had to admit she did look more presentable, and that boosted her confidence. The white fitted top clung to her and showed just a few centimetres of tanned, toned midriff, and the black and white vertical-striped loose trousers hugged her hips before flaring out over the pair of low wedge sandals she'd added. She was only on set as an observer today—it was a chance to get a feel for how things worked before her attendance was officially required and, because there were no stunts scheduled for today, she didn't need to be in clothes that would have to withstand an emergency.

She was met by George's assistant, Erica, who escorted her to the make-up trailer.

Oliver winked at her as she stepped inside and Kat's nervousness about being on set was replaced by the nervous excitement that she felt every time she saw him. It had been a long time since anyone had paid her some attention and she couldn't deny she found it extremely flattering.

In Coober Pedy all the locals knew her and she didn't really interact with the tourists, except when they needed her medical expertise. She preferred to be at home when she wasn't at work, but that habit wasn't conducive to meeting people. She couldn't remember the last time someone had asked her out.

'All done.' The make-up artist removed the disposable collar that protected Oliver's costume and he stood up. He was wearing a space suit, dirty and torn, and his make-up made him look as though he'd been through an ordeal, lost on an alien planet. He hadn't shaved, and Kat assumed he was supposed to look dishevelled, thirsty, and possibly in pain, but, to her eyes, he looked unbelievably good. The fake dirt and dust made his eyes even more noticeable, a more vivid blue.

'What are you filming today?'

'Do you know the plot?'

'Not really. George gave me a little overview but not a script. I know it's a science fiction movie but I have to admit that's not really my thing. I like romantic comedies.'

'I'll have to remember that. OK, the plot in a nutshell: Earth has set up a space station, an air force base in the sky, the first line of defence against alien attack. One space station has been badly damaged and we are supposed to be evacuating and returning to Earth, but my "ship" is hit and crash-lands on another, previously undiscovered, planet. I have a dozen crew on board. Mechanics, scientists, astronauts, physicists, defence. I'm the commander, the most senior defence person on the ship. The planet has an atmosphere but it's thin. Low oxygen—a bit like high altitude. There are no trees, nothing green, it's a barren place, but gas readings indicate moisture and we think there could be water somewhere. I've gone off to scout.

'I crash my vehicle and damage the windshield, so I'm affected by exposure to the heat and by altitude sickness. I lose consciousness and when I wake up I find myself in a cave. We're going to use the caves you showed George—it's been added to the schedule. I don't remember crawling into the cave but I see drag marks in the dirt. It looks like someone dragged me in, and then I notice cave drawings—signs of alien life. The cave goes deeper into the earth and I go as far as I can without any light, and I'm sure I can smell water.

'The scene we're filming this morning is a few days later; I'm feeling better and I've managed to fix the all-terrain vehicle. I still haven't seen any other life forms but in the film the audience knows I'm being watched by something, although they haven't seen anything yet either. I return to the spaceship, where I'm greeted very warmly by the leading lady, who thought I must have died.'

Oliver was smiling and Kat could imagine how that reunion scene was going to play out.

'That's Julia?'

'Yep,' he said as they reached the set. 'Grab a seat here,' he told her, indicating a chair next to George and handing her a pair of headphones so she could listen to the dialogue.

Filming began with Oliver arriving back at the spaceship. Julia's character saw the ATV approaching and came out of the spaceship to investigate.

The scene moved inside and Kat repositioned herself so that she could continue to watch on a screen.

Julia was playing a space soldier, Oliver's second-in-command. She had some medical training and had to attend to his injuries. She insisted that Oliver be quarantined and undergo a medical check-up. They were alone in the scene and Kat could feel herself blushing as Oliver's character stripped down to his underwear.

There were several screens in front of Kat, each showing a different angle. There was a wide shot and then close-ups of Julia and Oliver. Kat focused on the screen showing Oliver. She couldn't keep her eyes off him. He drew her in...the incredible colour of his eyes, the intense look on his face. She felt as if he was looking directly at her, even though she knew he wasn't. She could see why he was such a star. He was gorgeous, charismatic.

The scene intensified. Julia's character leant towards Oliver and then they were kissing. Kat felt hot and flustered, unsure where to look. It felt voyeuristic but she couldn't look away. She wondered what it would be like to be Julia.

The scene had taken most of the morning to film and in between takes Oliver chatted to the cast and crew. Kat could see why women fell for him: he was nice to everyone. Finally, they broke for lunch and Oliver came and sat beside her. He had stripped off his costume and was wearing a pair of shorts and a T-shirt now, his character's persona discarded with his clothes.

'Are you OK? You're not bored?' he asked.

'Not at all. I'm used to sitting around, waiting. As a paramedic it's part of my job description; we're happy when things are quiet. And this is a far more interesting way to pass the time.' It was exciting. The whole experience was a novelty. She wasn't bored, far from it, although she was a little bit jealous. 'Julia seems to have recovered from her crisis of the other night,' she said.

'For now. Let's hope things have calmed down on that front, although I doubt it.'

'What happened?'

'Her husband had an affair. Julia didn't want to work on this movie, she didn't want to leave him alone, but she was contractually obligated, so she's not happy that she has to be here, so far away from home. I think George has promised to fly her husband out here but it remains to be seen if he'll turn up. This movie could save my reputation and end her marriage, so I understand why she's upset, but the less drama we have, the quicker filming is wrapped here and the sooner she can get home to the States.'

'She didn't look like she was missing her husband during those scenes.'

Oliver laughed. 'That's the idea. She's a good actress.'

'Are you sure that's all it is?'

'Are you jealous?'

'No,' she lied.

'Believe me, it's all acting. I may have a reputation of romancing my leading ladies but not the married ones, and I'm really trying to clean up my image. I don't need any rumours circulating. If she wants revenge I'm not the one who's going to oblige. I don't want to get into any arguments with irate husbands. I do have empathy for her, though; I've been cheated on before and it's not a good position to be in. It's bad enough going through something like that in private, but when your disastrous love-life gets splashed across the tabloids it makes you wary. I feel for her but I can't afford to make her problems mine—I've got enough of my own.'

Oliver picked up their plates and took them back to the serving counter, leaving Kat to wonder who cheated on him and why. Had it made him more careful about his affairs?

It didn't seem so if the tabloids were to be believed, but there were always two sides to a story. Maybe his romances were just casual, or for publicity. That would be one way to protect yourself from heartache. She wondered what it would be like not knowing who you could trust.

'Are you staying a bit longer?' he asked when he returned. 'Do you want to watch more filming? The next scene involves some of the other characters, while I'm missing, presumed dead.'

'Do you always film out of sequence?' Kat asked; she hadn't imagined it happening like that.

'More often than not, I guess we do, but it depends on a lot of things.'

'Like what?'

'Weather and location mostly. Or sometimes if an actor has to lose or gain weight or change their hairstyle through the movie…that will affect the order. It also might depend on who is required for the scene, if we need a lot of extras, things like that; they might be brought in for a few days to do all their scenes. Then, of course, there are always retakes, which can be difficult to manage, particularly if we've got other filming commitments for other projects. Would you like to watch? Otherwise we could hang out in my trailer?'

'I thought you didn't want any rumours.'

'Rumours with you I don't have an issue with—you're single and over the age of eighteen,' he said with a smile.

'With protective relations who spend their

days blowing things up for fun. Are you sure you want to take them on?'

'They blow things up for fun?'

'Yes, but it's legitimate. They're opal miners.'

'And they mine using explosives?'

'Sometimes.'

'OK, forewarned is forearmed, I guess. If you like I can show you the reels from the other day; you can see what the stunts look like and why the first-aid officer quit. No ulterior motive, I promise. I'll even leave the door open if it makes you feel more comfortable.'

'I can't believe you walked away without a scratch,' she said when she'd finished watching the footage. She had forced herself to concentrate but it had been difficult. They were sitting side by side on the couch, as it had the best view of the screen, but, while Oliver appeared relaxed, Kat was a bundle of nerves. She was super-aware of him beside her. She could feel him breathing, and every time he moved she braced herself in case he touched her. Each time he did her heart raced, her mouth went dry and her skin tingled.

'I had a few bruises and a headache but I'm fine.'

'Why on earth would you do your own stunts?'

'Because it's fun.'

'Don't you worry about getting hurt?'

'I've always loved testing my limits. My brother and I grew up in a house with very strict rules, thanks to our father, and I always enjoyed breaking them. I guess I thought of them more as recommendations.'

'What happened when you got caught?'

'We were punished, so I learnt the hard way to balance risk and reward. If I thought the risk wasn't worth the punishment I learnt to rein in my wild side. Stunts are calculated risks, mostly. The buzz I get from doing them outweighs the risk that something might go wrong. It's Chris's job, and yours, to keep me safe.'

'If Chris does his job right then you shouldn't need me,' she retorted. 'There's only so much I can do.'

Kat liked to follow the rules. She'd seen too many times the things that could go wrong when rules were broken.

There was a knock on the door and Oliver was summoned back to Make-Up and Wardrobe.

'We're filming a love scene this afternoon, so the set is closed,' he told her, 'but if you're free later, why don't you come back for dinner? I'm helping out on the grill.'

'I have an ambulance shift tonight.' She could have left it at that—he didn't know how things worked around here—but she found herself elaborating. 'But I can be on call. I'll let Dave know where I am and he can call me in if he needs me.'

'Are you sure? I don't want to be held responsible if you're needed.'

'Positive. As long as I'm contactable it's fine.'

She had intended to heed George's warning and resist Oliver's charms, but it was harder than she'd anticipated. It was one thing to tell herself that she could resist him when she was home alone, but quite another when he greeted her with a big smile and laughter in his blue eyes. He was charming and irresistible and she suspected it was only a matter of time before he would win her over.

CHAPTER THREE

KAT PUSHED OPEN the door to the police station and squeezed herself inside. It looked as if the whole town had come running when the cry for help had gone out, and the small station was bursting at the seams. She'd been getting ready to go back to the film set for dinner when she'd received a call telling her that a missing person report had come in. She had called Oliver with her apologies and headed for the station. Unfortunately, a missing backpacker trumped her other plans. She searched the crowd for her cousins, knowing they would be in the thick of the action, as she wondered if she'd get another dinner date. No, not a date, she reminded herself, an invitation.

She'd just spotted her cousins when she heard someone calling her name. She turned around to find Oliver coming through the door behind her.

'Oliver! What are you doing here?'

'Well, I thought your excuse was either the best rejection I'd ever received, or if it was true we figured you could use some help.'

'We?'

Kat looked at the men filing in behind him and saw that Oliver had brought Chris and some of the crew with him.

'Someone has gone missing?' he asked.

'Pietro Riccardo, an Italian backpacker, has been reported missing by his girlfriend. He went noodling—fossicking for opal,' Kat clarified when she saw several confused expressions, 'on his own. The girlfriend didn't go with him because she had a headache, and Pietro hasn't come back. There's a public noodling area in the centre of town but he's not there. The police have called the hotels, bars, pubs and clubs, thinking he might have just stopped for a drink, but he's not at any of those either. We have to start spreading the search.'

'Is there something we can do? Can we help?'

'If you'd like to, thank you. I'll see if I can get you assigned to my search party.'

'You're searching? You're not taking the ambulance?'

Kat shook her head. 'The crew who were already on shift will stay at the station. We don't know which way Pietro's gone, so there's no point sending the ambulance off in one direction, only for them to have to turn around and head a different way. We'll split up into search parties, and the search will be coordinated by the Coober Pedy mine rescue team.'

'You're telling me this happens often enough that you have an official search and rescue unit?'

'Yes. There are enough accidents on the mines with both miners and locals that we are needed fairly often.' Kat and her cousins were all members of the team. 'We're assuming the missing backpacker is injured, which is why he hasn't returned of his own accord, but there's also a high possibility that he's fallen down a disused mine shaft.'

'Are there really exposed mine shafts around here?'

'Of course. There are thousands of them. You've seen the warning signs, haven't you?'

'The signs that say "Don't Run", "Deep Shafts", "Don't Walk Backwards"?'

'Yes.'

'Those signs are serious? They're not just for the tourists to take selfies with?'

'They're definitely serious. We're not on a movie set; this is real.'

Oliver frowned. 'And just how often do people fall down mine shafts?'

'More often than you'd think and far more often than we'd like. You were told to watch where you walk around town, weren't you?'

'Yes. But I didn't really think about why.'

'Luckily for you most of the shafts in town have been covered over. It's just once you get out of town you need to be careful. People have gone missing and never been found. It's presumed they're down a hole somewhere. It's a perfect way to get away with murder.'

'You're kidding.'

'I'm not actually, but don't worry, that doesn't happen as much now. It's not the wild west it once was out here. People are a little more law-abiding.'

'OK, let me get this straight. We're going to be wandering around, in the dark, looking down old mine shafts.'

'He could be anywhere, and he might not be down a mine shaft, but if you're worried, no one will mind if you back out.'

'I'm not backing out. I offered to help and unless I'm going to be in the way I'm happy to be another pair of eyes.'

'The more people we have searching the better. Pietro didn't take his car, which is good and bad. Bad because we can't search for the car, which would be easier to find, good because it means he needs to be within walking distance of town, but bad again because we don't know in which direction he's gone and his mobile phone either isn't on, is flat or is out of service range.' She broke off as she was approached. 'Hey, Dave. Oliver, this is Dave Reed, another paramedic. Dave, this is Oliver Harding; he and some of the cast and crew from the movie have offered to help search.'

'Good to meet you; appreciate the help.' Dave was his normal, relaxed self; good in a crisis, he was one of Kat's favourite colleagues. They had been rostered on together for the night shift until the missing-person report changed their plans. Dave and Oliver shook hands as the crowd was silenced so instructions could be given.

They were spilt into search parties to head out of town in all directions. Kat took Oliver with her and they joined Dean and Roger. She was glad to be in the same search party as her cousins, not only because of their search and rescue skills but also because they were experienced miners who were fit and strong, but she was a little concerned about whether they would see Oliver as a valuable asset or as a liability. She'd been aware of them watching her as she'd spoken with Oliver and she hoped they didn't make him uncomfortable. As far as she was concerned, he was welcome to join them, and she didn't need her cousins to run interference on her behalf.

They collected their torches and Dave also handed Kat a backpack full of supplies that he had collected from the ambulance station on his way.

'What about tracker dogs?' Oliver asked after he'd offered to carry Kat's backpack and hoisted it onto his shoulders.

'The police force doesn't have tracker dogs, and the Aboriginal trackers we do have said the ground is too dry and there are too many prints in town to follow. If they knew which direction Pietro went in then maybe they'd have a chance, but,' she shrugged, 'we'll just have to walk and hope.'

Their group headed south, walking in a long line, side by side. They were supposed to spread out, swinging their lights in an arc several metres to either side of them, but Oliver kept bunching up, walking nearer to Kat, staying close to her. She wasn't sure if it was deliberate or if he wasn't aware that he was doing it, but she was very aware. He was quiet, there were no jokes, no banter, so he appeared to be taking this seriously, but she was still super-conscious of him.

The desert night was quiet and still, the air clear and cold. The sun had long since set, taking the heat of the day with it. The search party continued their slow and steady pace, taking it in turns to call Pietro's name.

'Are you sure his girlfriend was at the hostel?' Oliver asked after several minutes of silence. 'They didn't have an argument and she saw an opportunity to get rid of him?'

Kat laughed. 'I don't think she's a suspect and I think you've got an overactive imagination!'

'Maybe I've read too many movie scripts, but there's always a twist in the tale.'

They were into the second hour of the search, when Pietro was finally located, injured but alive, at the bottom of a disused mine shaft.

Oliver sat on a rock in a desert in the middle of South Australia and listened to the experienced rescuers plan Pietro's extraction from the mine shaft. There were literally thousands of mine shafts, as Kat had told him, and he'd thought it was an impossible task to find someone who could have fallen into one, so had been amazed when Pietro had actually been tracked down. The whole situation was surreal.

He listened to Pietro's apologies echoing up from the shaft. Oliver felt for the guy. He sounded embarrassed. It turned out he was a doctor, in Australia on a three-month holiday before he was due to return to Italy to start his surgical residency. He was mortified that he had sustained an injury and needed rescuing, but Oliver thought he should be grateful that he'd been found, that the people of Coober Pedy knew what to do.

But even Oliver couldn't believe what he heard next. What those same people were planning on doing. Or, more to the point, who was going to be doing it. He stood up and approached Kat, forgetting in his consternation that he probably should stay out of the way and that this retrieval had nothing to do with him.

'What are you doing?' he asked. 'You're not going down there?' The shaft was pitch black, the opening narrow, maybe only three feet wide, but the drop to the bottom was deep. When they had shone their torches down hundreds of these while looking for Pietro, Oliver had got the impression that this was what the mines looked like until Kat had explained that a lot of these narrow shafts were from exploratory drilling. If opal traces, or anything that had potential, was found the miners would excavate further. They might go down the hole for a look but most of the mines were now open cut using big machines. But it seemed as though Kat was about to descend into this darkness.

'Of course I am,' Kat replied. 'Someone has to. That shaft is over thirty feet deep. He says he's broken his ankle but he could have sustained more serious injuries. He needs to be assessed and then he needs to be brought up to the surface, which means he needs a harness. Someone has to attach that to him. There's not much room, and I'm the only one with the right experience who will fit.'

'Is it safe? It won't collapse?'

'It's sandstone. The same rock we build our houses with. It's safe enough. You don't need to worry —I've done this before. It's no more dangerous than when you do your own stunt work. Probably safer. You're not worried because I'm a woman, are you?'

'No, of course not. I work with stunt women all the time, and I know they're as capable as men.' But he was worried because it was Kat.

'I'm trained for this. I'll be fine,' she told him as she stepped into a harness.

Oliver watched, his heart in his mouth, as Kat's cousin Roger checked the harness. He had to trust that Kat knew what she was doing but that didn't mean he had to like it. He didn't want anything to happen to her before he got a chance to know her better. He had never met anyone like her and the more time they spent together the more fascinating he found her. She looked like a supermodel but seemed completely unaware of how stunning she was. She was smart and sexy but with an unusual air of innocence. He knew he had to be careful. She didn't seem as wise in the ways of the world as the women he normally mixed with, and he'd seen how her cousins kept one eye on her at all times—which meant they had one eye on him too tonight, which, he had to admit, made him a little uncomfortable, but he was respectful, and despite what the tabloids said about him that had always been his way.

A winch on the front of the four-by-four police vehicle lowered Kat into the hole. Oliver didn't think he breathed once until, after what seemed like a lifetime, she finally emerged again. With Pietro strapped to her.

Oliver wanted to rush over to her to make sure she was OK but this was not about the two of them and this time he forced himself to wait in the background as Kat, Dave and the other paramedics, who had arrived with the ambulance, attended to their patient. He felt like a teenage schoolboy longing to be noticed, but he was prepared to wait.

Eventually, as Pietro was being loaded into the ambulance, Kat came over to him. 'I'm sorry, I have to go. Pietro's English is good but his Italian is better. I speak Italian,' she said with a shrug, 'so I've offered to go with him to the hospital.'

'Of course.' Oliver didn't have any expectations that they'd get time together tonight; he realised that her job came first. Much like his. He couldn't object to that.

'Thank you for your help. I'm sorry I couldn't make it to dinner.'

'That's OK. I've got tomorrow off. If you're free we could reschedule till then.'

She hesitated and he prepared himself for the brush-off, but she surprised him when she said, 'I'd like that. But, assuming the rest of my shift is quiet, why don't I pick you up in the morning? I have a place I'd like you to see. Can you be ready early? Say, eight o'clock?'

Saskia was ready and waiting when the ambulance pulled up at the hospital.

'This is Pietro Riccardo...'

Kat pushed the stretcher through the emergency doors as she listened to Dave's summary of Pietro's suspected injuries, most of which Saskia knew from the phone call they'd made en route, and then the summary of treatment so far.

'Put him in the first cubicle. Damien is already here; we'll get him sorted,' Saskia told them, before turning her attention to the patient. 'Hello, Pietro, my name is Saskia.'

'Italian is his first language,' Kat told her before translating for Pietro. 'Saskia is a nurse and this is our doctor, Damien,' Kat continued the introductions as they wheeled Pietro into a treatment bay. 'They're going to do a more thorough assessment and I'll stay to translate if you need me to, OK?'

'Grazie.'

'Are you in pain?'

Pietro was still clutching the little green Penthrax whistle but he shook his head.

Despite the pain relief he seemed quite capable of following the proceedings and understanding what Damien and Saskia were saying—perhaps due to his medical training the English words didn't sound too unfamiliar—but Kat stayed with him until he was taken for X-rays.

He was lucky. He had a fracture dislocation of his left ankle which needed surgery and a suspected ligament tear in his right shoulder, but he'd escaped more serious injury.

'I want him to have some detailed scans of his lower back, head and right shoulder, but I think he's been relatively fortunate,' Damien said as he reviewed the plain X-rays, which was all they were equipped to take at the Coober Pedy hospital. 'We'll need to call the flying doctor and get him transferred to Adelaide. Is he travelling with someone?'

'His girlfriend,' Kat said. 'She should be here—someone was going to collect her from the backpackers' hostel.'

Kat explained what was happening to Pietro while Saskia got him comfortable, and then she and Kat left him dozing while they waited for the retrieval team.

'So, I hear Oliver helped with the search,' Saskia said as she made them coffee.

'How did—?' Kat began to ask before realising she already knew the answer. 'Dean told you.'

Saskia just grinned in reply.

'What else did he say?'

'Nothing much.'

Kat knew that wouldn't be true. 'C'mon, Sas, Dean always has an opinion about any man in my life.'

She knew she'd made a mistake as soon as she'd finished the sentence and if she'd hoped Saskia had missed it she was out of luck.

Saskia almost spat out her coffee. 'I knew it! You like him. Not that anyone could blame you—there's a reason Oliver Harding has been voted the world's sexiest man. Twice.'

'I said *any* man.'

'You say tomato…' Saskia was still grinning. 'Dean said that Oliver couldn't keep his eyes off you.'

'He said that?' Kat felt a warm glow.

'Mmm-hmm.' Saskia considered her. 'So, you like him.' It wasn't a question.

'I do. But—'

'No buts—'

'But you know how people talk in this town.'

'You worry too much about what people think. Besides, you're twenty-seven, you're a grown woman, you're your own boss.'

'That's not exactly true. You know what it's like when you've grown up here—everyone has an opinion on how you live your life.'

'Well, all I'm saying is that he seems keen and it would be a shame to let this opportunity go to waste. If it's not you spending time with him, it will be someone else. Is that what you want?'

No. She didn't want that.

'You don't have to marry the guy,' Saskia continued. 'Don't overthink things, just have some fun. Oliver looks like he knows how to have fun. How long is he here for?'

'Only a few weeks.'

'If you're worried about what people think

I'm sure you could manage to be discreet for that long. Treat it like a holiday romance.'

'I'm not looking for a holiday romance. I'm looking for the person I'm going to spend the rest of my life with. What's the point of starting something that can go nowhere?'

'Are you kidding? The point is there's a man in town who has literally been voted the sexiest man alive and who seems to have taken a fancy to you. You've been bemoaning the lack of men here for months. Are you seriously telling me you'd pass up this opportunity? With a man who looks like he does? You must be crazy.'

She wasn't crazy but she was scared. Scared she wouldn't be able to control things. He had awakened her senses, he was making her feel things she hadn't felt in a long time. He made her laugh. He made her nervous. Excited. Happy. She liked him, really liked him, but she was worried things would get complicated. Coober Pedy was a small town. How could she expect to have fun without everyone else knowing her business? Could she keep him separate from her everyday life? She didn't need to be the centre of town gossip or to have any interference from her family.

Had she made a mistake by asking him to spend the day with her tomorrow?

Maybe she had, but she didn't want to change her mind. She had planned to take him away from town; she wanted to show him the wildness and beauty of her world. She could still do that. She had the perfect spot in mind. A place where she doubted they would see another soul.

Oliver was waiting in front of the hotel when Kat turned off the main street and climbed out of her dusty four-by-four. She was wearing a T-shirt and a pair of very short denim cut-offs. She looked amazing, but that wasn't enough to keep his attention. He was completely distracted by the canoe that was strapped to the roof of her car.

'Now I think I've seen everything,' he said as he kissed her cheek. She smelt of soap and sunshine. 'What on earth have you got planned for us? I thought we only had a few hours.'

'We do.'

'So the canoe is just for show?'

'You'll have to wait and see. Did you get my message?' she said as she looked him over. 'Did you bring something to swim in?'

'I did. But you have me intrigued. A canoe and a bathing suit. I flew into Coober Pedy and I don't remember seeing any water for about four hundred miles.'

'You weren't looking in the right places,' she said as they got into the car and slammed the doors. 'The name Coober Pedy means boys' waterhole.'

'Does it? I was told it meant white man in a hole.'

'That's sort of true. In the local Aboriginal culture a boy is a male who hasn't been through an initiation ceremony. There was a waterhole for those boys near here. The Pitjantjatjara word for white man is the same as for boy, as neither of them have been initiated, so some people translated it as "white man's waterhole" as opposed to "boy's water hole", and somewhere along the line it became "white man in a hole".'

They headed east out of town, past the never-ending mullock heaps that dotted the landscape—piles of dirt that had been dug out of the earth in the quest for opal—past numerous damaged, abandoned cars and dead animals that were decaying on the side of the road.

'The two often go hand in hand,' Kat said when Oliver commented on the roadside carnage. 'People don't drive according to the conditions. You shouldn't really drive at night out here if it can be avoided. Cattle, emus, kangaroos, even wombats can do a lot of damage to your car if you hit one of them, particularly at speed. We have a high number of fatal accidents.'

'But why don't the cars get towed?'

'Most do eventually,' she said as they drove past a utility vehicle that was crumpled, bonnet compacted, windscreen smashed. Black skid marks could be seen across the road. 'That one was recent. Just a couple of weeks ago. The teenage driver swerved to avoid a cow, lost control and rolled the car.'

'Were you here?'

She nodded. 'Dave and I were on shift.'

'Was everyone all right?' he asked as he kept his eyes on the wreck.

'No. There was a fatality. A boy had been riding in the tray of the ute—he was thrown out and died at the scene. Another was in a critical condition and was evacuated by the flying doctor, and two more were taken to the local hospital.'

'I can't imagine doing your job. It must be tough. How do you cope with it?'

'It's a rewarding job. I like feeling as though I'm making a difference. Even with that accident, the fatality was dreadful, a terrible waste of a young life, but Dave and I managed to keep the other boy alive until the flying doctor got here. I've seen so many accidents like this, so you take the good with the bad, but it's why I like to follow the rules, not break them. Life isn't something that should be taken for granted.'

He remembered her comment about him doing his own stunts and wondered if she would accuse him of taking life for granted. He didn't take it for granted but he did think that life was for living and he wasn't going to sit around and watch other people living their lives. He wanted to be a participant.

Kat slowed her car and turned off the road onto a smaller dirt track. The faded signpost read *Lake Cadibarrawirracanna.*

'There's a lake out here?'

Kat nodded. 'A salt lake.'

'Does the name have a meaning?'

'It does. It means *stars dancing on the water.*'

'It sounds beautiful,' he said, although he didn't think it actually would be. He couldn't picture a lake in this barren landscape. Not even his active imagination could envision that.

'It is. I wanted you to see the beauty in the desert. You just need fresh eyes.'

'Wow.' They crested a small rise and Oliver was stunned at the sight of a vast lake, shimmering silver in the sun, before them. It stretched for miles across the flat landscape, a few trees clinging to its edges. A flock of birds rose off the water and took to the sky, startled by the sound of the engine, but other than that there was nothing else but land, water and sky. Now that the birds had flown he couldn't see another living thing except for him and Kat.

Kat parked in the shade of a stand of trees and he helped her lift the two-man canoe from the roof of the car.

'Do you want to take the canoe out on the lake?' she asked as she passed him a blanket and some cushions from the back of the car.

Oliver spread the blanket on the sand. He didn't want to paddle just now. He wanted to just sit and take in the view. And Kat.

'Later, I think. I can't remember the last time I sat and did nothing. I'm usually doing a movie, learning lines for a movie, doing publicity, interviews, going to red carpet events.'

'Or going to parties.'

Something in her tone put him on alert. 'Have you been reading about me?'

'A little,' she admitted.

'Don't believe everything you read.'

'George told me the same thing. That's why I thought I'd ask you; you can tell me what was and wasn't true.'

'Such as?' he asked, although he was pretty

sure he knew what she would have read and what subject she would be interested in.

'Did a girl overdose and die at a party at your house? Is that true?'

'Yes.' He wasn't surprised by her question, that story was currently the first thing that popped up if someone did an internet search on his name.

'What happened?'

'I'm not one hundred per cent sure. I was away; I was in New Orleans working on a film and had friends staying in my house. They held a party. From what the police told me the girl who overdosed allegedly brought the drugs with her, something went wrong and she died.'

'You weren't there?'

'No, but it was my house, so I was linked by association. My publicist and agent thought it would be a good idea to keep me out of Hollywood for a bit longer while it was investigated so they sent me here. I thought it was probably a good idea too but this time I haven't left any friends staying there. I used to host a lot of parties, but I'm rethinking that scene now. I'm going to make some changes to my lifestyle when I get home. This trip down under will give me a chance to reset.' He stood up; he didn't want to talk about his old life any longer, and he was telling the truth when he said he was thinking about making changes. It was time to start behaving more responsibly. He was thirty-two years old; he couldn't continue his partying ways for ever. 'How about that paddle now?'

They worked up an appetite taking the canoe out on the lake, but Kat had anticipated that and had packed a picnic.

'Where did you get all of this on a Sunday morning?' Oliver asked as she unpacked cold meats and fruit from an ice box.

'I raided the pantry. My family is Italian. Someone is always in the kitchen making something or preserving something. I have my father's salami, my aunt Rosa's sun-dried tomatoes, my cousin's wife's bread,' she said as she handed him a loaf of bread.

'This bread smells fresh—surely that wasn't in the pantry?'

'No, Maya, that's Roger's wife, made it this morning. She lives next door.'

'Next door?'

'Yes. My whole family lives in the same street. In the same hill.'

'That sounds a bit close for comfort.'

Kat shrugged. 'It's how it's always been.'

'I'd love to see inside an underground house.'

She was tempted to invite him to hers but there was bound to be someone around. If not her father, it would be her aunt or cousins. 'It's not so different to your hotel. We have front doors, front windows, electricity, running water. It's just on a smaller scale than the hotel.'

'What happens if you're claustrophobic?'

'I don't know. It doesn't bother me. The rooms are light and ventilated. We have skylights and air vents. You must have noticed all the metal shafts poking up out of the hills in town. Those are ventilation shafts. They're wrapped with wire to stop the snakes entering through them.'

'And it's safe? The houses don't collapse?'

'The rock around here is sandstone, and it's very stable—we can excavate large spaces without needing structural support. We've got some enormous underground spaces in town. The Serbian church and a couple of the museums are massive. If you want to see a house, Faye's is open to tourists.'

'You're not going to invite me over?'

'It's not my house. It's my father's.'

'You still live with your parents?'

She felt the familiar pang at the mention of parents. 'I live with my father,' she clarified. 'My mother died a few years ago.'

'I'm sorry, Kat. How old were you?'

'Twenty-two. She was killed in a car accident.'

'Out here?'

She nodded. The memories were still painful. Her feelings of guilt still high. 'A bus had been sitting behind a truck, trying to overtake, the driver got impatient and pulled out over double white lines to have a look, and my mother was driving in the opposite direction. He smashed into my mother's car. It was his fault, he didn't obey the road rules, but he survived, while my mother died at the scene.

'I came back here after she died to be with my dad. And I'm still here. I am the single daughter of an Italian father. We don't move out until we get married.' Her family owned a lot of land and the only thing that would change when she married was that her father and uncle and cousins would dig her a house next to the rest of them, but Oliver had sounded so shocked she didn't think he needed to hear that too.

'How old were you when you left home?' she asked. Oliver was watching her closely and she wondered if he was going to let her change the subject. She hoped so; she didn't want to talk about her mother, she didn't want to be sad. She breathed a sigh of relief as Oliver followed her lead.

'I went to college in California when I was seventeen. My parents were in Japan.'

'You went to college? To study acting?'

'Actually, no. I went to law school. Acting wasn't considered a career and one of my father's sons was always expected to go into the defence force. My brother refused, so that left me. I had no intention of joining the force either so I enrolled in law school under the pretence that I could join the armed forces that way. But once I got to college, I realised I had visions of myself as a lawyer standing in front of a court room arguing cases. Performing, I suppose. Much like what you see in the movies. *That's* what I wanted to do. So I joined the drama clubs and I found I had a talent for it, so then I started auditioning for movie roles and when I got my first one I dropped out of law school. My father has barely spoken to me since.'

'Because you didn't join the army?'

'Because I am a disappointment and he disapproves of my career choice. Because I chose acting over fighting.'

'And what about your mother? What did she think?'

'My mother is the daughter of an army general and now a wife of an army general. She followed orders.'

'What?'

'Orders *might* be the wrong word,' Oliver said, but to Kat's ears it sounded as if it was exactly what he meant, 'but she certainly never questioned Dad's decisions. Never argued. I can't say that I blame her. Isaac and I learnt that lesson early on too. The moment we were old enough we left home. It was the only way we could do what we wanted. Our mother didn't have that option.'

'How often do you see your parents?'

'I don't visit. I speak to my mother when my father's not around. She believes her loyalty is to her husband, but I think she's happy if I'm happy.'

'And are you happy?' Kat couldn't imagine being happy without her family.

'Yes. I get to experience all kinds of things; I travel the world pretending to be other people and giving people an escape from their everyday lives, from the world. I'm having fun.'

'So, what's next for you, after this movie?'

'I would love to have a role in a musical. I've done comedy, action, romantic leads, but I'd love an opportunity to try something new. I'd be the next Hugh Jackman if I could. You know, he started on the stage in musicals.'

'Can you sing?'

'Not well.'

'Dance?'

'Not as well as I sing,' he laughed. 'But dancing I can learn. Growing up, I wasn't allowed to have dancing lessons. It wasn't something boys did. Of course the more I was told I couldn't do something the more I wanted to. Would you like to come dancing with me?'

'In Coober Pedy? There aren't a lot of places to dance around here.'

'All you need is some music and a willing partner. Actually, music is optional. We could dance right now if you wanted to.'

Kat had learnt by now that Oliver didn't take anything seriously. His life was all about fun. In comparison, she took *everything* seriously.

He was making her nervous. Not in a bad way, but she was worried that he was going to convince her to dance and she didn't think she'd be able to handle that. She knew being in his arms would be her undoing.

She stood up.

'Are we going to dance?' he asked.

She shook her head and reached for the ice box. 'No, we need to get going. I've got to get back—I'm going to my cousin's for dinner.' She tidied up the remains of their picnic, picked up their glasses and packed them away.

'The one who lives next door?'

'Yes.'

'You're having dinner together again?'

'It's kind of a weekly ritual.'

'Really? Wouldn't you rather stay here with me?' He was standing now too. He lifted her hair and tucked it over her shoulder. His fingers skimmed her flesh, making it hum where he touched her. He was standing close and his eyes were mesmerising. He was engaging, funny, charming and incredibly good-looking, and Kat was tempted but she didn't give in.

'I'm expected there.'

'And do you always do what's expected?'

'Pretty much.' Following the rules and doing what was expected was part of her personality, but circumstances had also influenced her behaviour. She'd seen death and disaster first hand, and growing up in such a harsh environment had tainted her perceptions of what she could get away with.

'That's a pity. We could have fun.'

She'd forgotten what it was like to have fun. To have dreams.

'You're blushing,' he said. 'Do you think I'm flirting with you?

Kat didn't reply. She couldn't. Oliver was

standing so close, with his hand on her arm, and his proximity stripped her of the capability of speech.

'You should,' he added. 'I am.' He grinned, his slow smile stretching from one corner of his gorgeous mouth to the other.

'Why on earth would you want to flirt with me?'

'Because you are incredibly beautiful.'

She laughed. She wanted to believe him but she couldn't. 'You must have met hundreds of women who are more beautiful than me.'

'I can honestly say I haven't met one as beautiful as you who hasn't had any help. So either you have an amazing surgeon and I am a blind fool or you are naturally stunning.'

'I am ordinary.'

'I disagree. You are beautiful and interesting. A little mysterious. It's like finding a pearl or a diamond out of place. A thing of beauty in a hostile environment.'

'I think I'm more like an opal. Tough and at home in the outback.'

'Perhaps, but that definitely makes you unique, which makes you more interesting. At least to me. My father moved us around the world when I was growing up and for the past twelve years I've continued to travel in the world of showbiz, but I don't get to meet many people like you. You fascinate me. Your background, the career you've chosen, the fact that you look so unexpected out here and yet you seem so comfortable. Content. Everyone I meet is competing for something—the next part, the next girl, the next dollar. You're refreshing.'

'And you are a flatterer.'

'Is it working?'

Yes, she thought, but that's not what she said. 'Not yet. You'll have to try a bit harder. I'm not that sort of girl.'

She suspected that, where Oliver was concerned, she might be exactly that type of girl, but she would make him work just a little bit harder. It wouldn't do him any harm.

He bent his head, brushing his lips over her ear, and she almost gave in then and there. Could he feel it? she wondered. Could he feel her self-control slipping?

'Well, I'm not going to give up and, to be fair, I have warned you, the more I'm told I can't have something, the more I want it.'

He was teasing her, testing her, and she knew she would eventually give in. She didn't have a hope in hell of resisting him for ever.

CHAPTER FOUR

KAT WAS ON set early for her first official day of duty. The sun was still rising in the east and the morning light streaked the sky with pink and gold and turned the earth a muted red. The landscape looked as though it had been touched up by an artist's brush using all the colours of an Aboriginal painting—ochre, gold, crimson, scarlet and the pink of a galah's feathers. The view was incredible and Kat hoped the colours would be captured on screen.

She sat on a chair behind George. She could see Oliver on two different screens over the director's shoulder but, looking across the flat planes of the earth, she could also see him standing on top of the hill, waiting for his cue.

Her mind drifted as she waited for filming to begin. Once again, she found her thoughts returning to the day they'd spent together at the lake. She had been pleasantly surprised about what a good time she'd had. They had flirted and laughed but, more importantly, they had talked and talked. She had shared things with him that she hadn't talked about in a long time, things she had never talked to anyone except Saskia about. And Oliver had listened.

Kat was beginning to think that maybe they could have a relationship that had some substance to it. There was definitely an attraction between them and they shared a sense of humour, but was that enough to overcome the differences she also knew they had? He was worldly, charming, independent and liked to push the boundaries. She was sheltered, sensible, a nurturer and a rule-follower. He might think she was refreshing but she suspected he might soon be bored. She suspected that, in reality, she was too vanilla for him.

'Action.'

The command came through the headset she was wearing and jolted her back to the present.

She saw Oliver start walking. The land was dry, the earth hard-packed, but Oliver's feet were sinking into sand. She knew George wanted the effect of soft ground making it arduous going for Oliver's character, and the prop crew had added a deep layer of fine red sand to the hill, reminding Kat that, in Oliver's world, nothing was really as it seemed.

The camera zoomed in and Kat switched her attention to the screen. She couldn't look away as the camera focused in on Oliver's face. His blue eyes were electric against the rose gold of the sky.

He continued to trudge across the ground and she could see him scanning the horizon and then, suddenly, he disappeared from the screen.

Kat heard her sharp intake of breath and flicked her gaze back to the hill. Oliver was tumbling down, head first.

She knew this was a stunt but it looked so real. She saw Oliver bouncing off the ground and wondered if, or hoped, he was wearing protective padding. It looked dangerous. And painful. She didn't want to watch but she couldn't look away.

Her whole body was tense. Her hands were clenched into tight fists and she couldn't breathe. The whole stunt probably lasted twenty seconds but it felt like a lifetime before Oliver finally hit the bottom of the hill, landing with a thud. Kat imagined she could feel the air being forced out of his lungs.

She waited, still holding her breath, for him to get up. For him to move.

The set was quiet.

No one moved. No one spoke.

What were they waiting for?

Kat didn't know but one thing she did know was that Oliver still hadn't moved. Surely he should be up by now?

He must be hurt.

Winded. Injured. Unconscious.

He could be any of those things.

Her instincts kicked in. She leapt off her chair and dropped the headset onto the seat. She grabbed her backpack, which was at her feet, and took off across the red sand, sprinting as fast as she could over the stony ground, hoping someone would think to grab her heavier, second bag of equipment.

'Cut!'

She was halfway across the site when she heard George's direction. Were they still filming? Had she just ruined the scene? Was this all part of the action?

She didn't break stride. It was too bad if she'd ruined it. She didn't care. It would be much worse if their star was injured and she left him lying on the ground. She was going to do her job and she wasn't going to let anyone stop her.

She reached Oliver's side.

He still hadn't moved.

His eyes were closed but she could see his chest rising and falling. As she dropped her backpack in the dust and knelt beside him, he opened his eyes.

She looked into his piercing blue eyes. Was one pupil slightly more dilated than the other?

She placed one hand on his chest. 'Don't move.'

Kat's face swam into focus.

The first thing he noticed were her red lips. The rest of her was a little fuzzy around the edges. Maybe he was hurt worse than he thought.

'Are they still filming?' he asked.

'What?'

'Are they still filming? I'm supposed to get up and keep moving.' At least, that was what he thought he was supposed to do. His mind was a little hazy.

'They're not filming but you're not getting up until I've checked you out. You've just fallen down a hill and got the wind knocked out of you.'

'I was supposed to fall down the hill. It's called acting.'

He could see George and some of the crew approaching. He felt bruised and sore but there was no way he was going to lie meekly on the ground. It was time to get up. Kat's hand was on his chest, keeping him on the ground. He could stand if he wanted to—she wasn't putting any pressure on him, just a warning hold.

He lifted his head and felt the earth spin a little. There was a sharp, stabbing pain in his left side as he sat up and he struggled not to wince, hoping Kat didn't notice.

'Oliver! You're obviously hurt—lie down and let me check you out. What am I doing here if you're not going to listen to me?' It seemed she hadn't missed the grimace.

She insisted that he stay down while she examined him. She was obviously annoyed with him; he thought she was poking and prodding him a bit harder than was necessary. She made him breathe deeply, move his limbs and head this way and that. He managed to do everything she asked, albeit with some discomfort, but he was sure he wasn't badly injured.

Kat seemed to have a different opinion. 'I think you might have cracked a rib. You should go to the hospital for precautionary X-rays.'

'Is that really necessary, Kat?' George asked. 'Isn't there something you could do for him here? We're behind on filming already.'

'He's not in any condition to film any stunts until he gets checked,' Kat argued.

'What if I shuffle scenes so there is no more stunt work today? You can stay and supervise. If you think we're putting his health at risk I'll let you take him off for X-rays. But if he's managing he can have X-rays at the end of the day.'

'There's no crepitus, just tenderness and pain on inhalation.'

'I have no idea what that means.'

'I'm thinking out loud,' Kat said. 'It means that with strapping, some pain relief and anti-inflammatory medication he might be OK. Give me twenty minutes now—that's enough time for oral pain relief to kick in—and then we'll reassess.'

Oliver was able to strip his costume off with some assistance. His ribs were painful but he was determined not to give Kat any reason to cart him off to hospital. Once again he was semi-naked and being attended to, but this time it was Kat, not Julia, assessing his injuries. Unfortunately they were in a tent in the middle of the desert, surrounded by dozens of crew, and his injuries were real, which put a bit of a dampener on things.

Kat strapped his ribs and he managed to work through the rest of the day. He was stiff and sore as the day wore on but he didn't quit. Kat had watched him like a hawk and the moment they wrapped for the day she bundled him off to the hospital.

* * *

'Hello again, Oliver. This is a pleasant surprise.'

He recognised Saskia as he and Kat stepped through the doors into Emergency. 'I didn't realise you were a nurse,' he said, his hopes that he could talk his way out of an examination evaporating. He knew he wouldn't be able to convince both Kat and Saskia that he was fine.

He suffered through more tests with the doctor before he was sent for X-rays.

'You have a mild concussion,' he was informed. That made two this week, Oliver thought, but he kept that information to himself. 'But there's no apparent fracture,' Damien said when the X-rays were developed. 'That doesn't mean you can't have a small crack somewhere that's just not showing up, but there's no major skeletal damage. Just soft tissue—a sprain, some swelling and bruising. Ice packs, some pain relief and some anti-inflammatory meds should do the trick. Rest tonight and then movement as comfortable.'

'I can go back to work?'

Damien nodded.

'What about monitoring the concussion? He's staying at the Cave Hotel,' Saskia asked before looking knowingly at Kat and adding, 'Alone. Shouldn't he have some supervision?'

'You haven't got any nausea? Haven't vomited?' Damien asked.

'No,' Oliver replied. He wasn't going to consent to supervision or to being admitted to hospital. He had a dull headache but he wasn't going to jeopardise the movie or his career by appearing incapacitated. Besides, his vision had cleared.

'I'm not sure we can justify a bed,' Damien said, 'But if you feel unwell either come back in or call 000. That's the emergency number.'

'000 will just call Kat,' Saskia told him as Damien left them.

'That doesn't sound like a bad compromise.'

'No, it won't get me,' Kat said. 'I'm not working tonight.'

'Even better,' Saskia replied. 'Why don't you take Oliver with you now, Kat? You don't have anything else to do, do you? And that way you can keep an eye on him. Make sure he's OK.'

That sounded good to Oliver. 'I'll buy you dinner,' he offered.

'This isn't a date.'

'OK, but one day we'll have a proper date.'

He figured she could call it whatever she liked but he would treat it like a date.

It had been a long time since he'd asked a

woman on a date because he'd wanted to get to know her. He'd been burnt once and had since shied away from dating except when he needed to do it for publicity. It kept things simple. There were no expectations if it was purely a business arrangement. There was no chance of disappointment on either side if the 'date' was mutually beneficial, and if the night ended with the two of them between the sheets it had always been mutually agreed upon with no suggestion that it made the evening into anything more than what it had been.

But he was well aware that he needed to curtail his brief encounters, he needed to clean up his reputation and make an effort to redeem himself from a party-going playboy to a serious, eligible, respectable man. He needed to commit some time to getting to know someone on a deeper level, to having a conversation that was about more than what cocktail he could buy them or what they'd like for breakfast, and he could do much worse than spend that time with Kat. He had no problem with getting to know her better. And, at some point in the near future, he would get her to agree to go on a proper date with him, but for now he'd be happy with whatever time she would give him.

* * *

In the end Kat agreed to dinner. Her only other option was to take Oliver home with her to feed him, and she was *not* going to introduce him to her father. Introducing someone she was dating was difficult enough, let alone someone for whom she had no label.

She knew she was being silly. If he was just a friend she wouldn't hesitate. But how would she explain Oliver? A work colleague? A movie star? Someone from out of town? Any of those descriptions would do but they wouldn't hide the fact that she was attracted to him and she hated to think what her dad would do or say if he noticed. He always seemed to be of the opinion that no one was good enough for his daughter and it would be humiliating if he gave Oliver the third degree. Oliver had made his intentions clear; he was pursuing her, but he had no more serious intentions than that. If he got her into bed she was certain that would be the end of it. She definitely didn't need to introduce him to her father.

She'd dropped Oliver at his hotel to shower and change before she raced home to do the same, cursing Saskia and her meddling ways all the while. Although she couldn't be too cross. There was a lot to be said about spending an evening with Oliver Harding. Even the anticipation was exciting.

She'd thrown a few supplies into the back of her four-by-four before picking him up again and driving him a few hundred metres to the petrol station.

'Do you want me to fill up the tank for you?' he offered as she turned off the road.

'No, thank you. I'm good,' she replied as she parked the car in a space out the front. 'This is where we're having dinner.'

'A roadhouse?' He sounded offended. 'I offered to buy you dinner. I can afford something fancier than a roadhouse diner.'

'Trust me, it's good. It's owned by Dean's best friend and there's a private room out the back.'

'Do you have a connection to everyone in this town?'

'Pretty much.'

Oliver held the door for her as they entered the roadhouse. They were warmly welcomed and ushered out the back, where they had the space to themselves. He pulled her chair out for her as she sat. She liked the attention. They ordered pizzas and talked about the places Oliver had lived in and travelled to. Kat had been to Adelaide to study and she'd been to Sydney once. Her life experiences were totally different to his but he didn't make her feel inexperienced. He was an entertaining storyteller, even for an audience of one, and Kat enjoyed listening to his tales. He questioned her about her childhood, what it was like growing up in Coober Pedy, and got her to divulge her most interesting work stories. She felt as if they could talk all night.

He picked up the bill when it was delivered to their table but it seemed he wasn't ready to say goodnight just yet. 'It's only early. Don't you think you need to keep an eye on me a little longer? Shall we have coffee? Dessert?'

'We can have dessert at the next stop.' Kat was pleased that he didn't seem keen for the night to end. She had other plans for them.

'There's more than one thing to do in town on a Saturday night?'

She bristled. 'There's plenty. I'm just not sure how much you'll appreciate.'

'Relax. I'm kidding.'

She unlocked her car and climbed in as Oliver held the door for her. She reached into the back seat and handed him a baseball cap.

'What's this for?'

'Protection.'

He raised an eyebrow and smiled. 'For you or me?'

'You.'

'You sure do things differently out here,' he said as Kat pulled onto the main street and drove back through town, turning right at the far end and onto a dirt road. She drove past a chain link fence. On the other side was a large screen.

'We're going to the movies?' Oliver asked.

Kat nodded. 'Outback style.'

She handed over cash at the gate before driving in to the outdoor theatre and reversing into a spot.

To their left was a small building housing the projection unit which also doubled as the kiosk. A couple of long benches were bolted into the ground in front of the kiosk for any patrons who hadn't driven, but these had been ignored in favour of a few, more comfortable, deckchairs. The whole set-up was very basic. Money had recently been spent on a new screen but funds were desperately needed to upgrade the rest of the facilities.

Kat tuned the radio and opened her door.

'Are you sweet or savoury?' she asked.

'Sorry?'

'The dessert I promised you. I'll get us something from the shop.'

'My buy.'

'No—' she started to argue, but he cut her off.

'I was buying dinner. If this is dessert then technically it's still part of dinner.'

She looked at him. Even with the baseball cap he was recognisable. His clothes were too city. He was too neat and tidy, too well-groomed.

'Thanks, but let's call it movie snacks, not dessert, and let me go.'

'Why?'

'Because I think it's better if you stay out of sight.' He frowned and she could see she'd confused him. She couldn't blame him. He had no idea what movie they'd come to see. 'I don't want you to be hassled.'

'No one has bothered me since I got to Coober Pedy. I don't think anyone could care less that I'm in town.'

Kat believed him. The locals were, by and large, unfazed by anything that happened outside of their world. Coober Pedy was a popular filming location for everything from documentaries to local horror flicks to Hollywood blockbusters and the locals couldn't care less. The ones who made a living from the tourists might be the exception but, while they liked the additional revenue that a film crew

and any associated publicity might bring, even they wouldn't make a nuisance of themselves by hassling the stars. The locals were focused on making money, making a living, surviving. Movies being made in town was a good drawcard for tourists, which made the town money. That was all the locals worried about, so she wasn't surprised that they were leaving the movie contingent alone, but the tourists in town might be a different story.

'Most of the town, probably not. But the people who are here tonight might. The first movie is one of yours.'

'One of mine? Which one?'

This Is War.' She waited to see if he was going to object. 'Do you mind watching one of your own? We're a bit limited for choice out here. There's a different double feature every Saturday night and tonight it's one of yours, but we could come back later for the second movie if it's a problem.'

Oliver glanced over his shoulder at the mound of pillows in the back of the car. 'If we stay, do I get to lie in the back with you and fool around?'

'Yes, to the first—'

'I know how this movie ends,' he interrupted with one of his slow smiles; 'you can afford to miss it—I can catch you up later.'

Kat laughed. 'My point *was*, that I will get the snacks because you're bound to be recognised here and I don't think it will make for a relaxing experience.'

'Relaxing in the back of your car with you was exactly the experience I had in mind.'

Kat raised her eyebrow and gave an exaggerated sigh. 'Sweet or savoury?'

'Surprise me.'

'Make yourself comfortable,' she said as she hopped out.

She returned with an armload of sweets and some cans of soft drink, passing everything to Oliver before climbing into the back. 'Take your pick. I have popcorn or FruChocs.'

'Fruit chocs?'

'FruChocs—chocolate-covered apricot balls. You have to try one. I've got beer too,' Kat said as she popped open a can, 'but you should probably steer clear of that if you've got a headache.'

'My headache seems to have gone,' he grinned. 'I'm feeling much better.'

The opening credits started to roll and Kat settled back. She was looking forward to the movie; it was a romantic comedy, which was much more her style than science fiction, but she knew she'd be happy to see anything that Oliver was in and was more than happy to be

curled up in the dark with him. He had rear-
ranged the pillows, making more of a semi-
circle, encouraging the two of them into the
middle of the car, like a little nest. She had to
sit close, their shoulders and thighs touching.
She didn't mind that at all.

She enjoyed the movie. At some point she
felt Oliver's arm wrap around her shoulder.
She was tucked against his side in the dark.
Despite the fact they were surrounded by other
cars, it had felt secluded and private and the
nervous tension she usually felt when she was
around him had dissipated. Maybe it was because she couldn't see him, but she was still
aware of him. The nervous tension had been
replaced by a heightened awareness. She had
felt every movement he'd made, every breath
he'd taken.

She'd felt his fingers twirling the ends of
her hair and making tiny patterns on her bare
shoulders. Her skin had come alive under his
touch and she felt as if she could have stayed
there for ever, cocooned with him in a world
of their own.

'What did you think?' he asked as the final
credits started to roll.

The film had made her cry. And laugh.
And, not that she'd admit it, she'd got a little
turned on in the sex scenes. 'I thought you

were great,' she said, grateful for the darkness as it hid the fact she was blushing.

'You don't have to be nice. It's OK if you thought it was terrible.' He was looking at her, his blue-eyed gaze bright even in the dim light. He was smiling. She wondered if he was always happy.

'No, really, it was fun, but do you find it weird watching yourself on screen?' She had wondered if he'd enjoy it or find it uncomfortable.

'A bit. I tend to focus on everyone else's characters. Especially in the sex scenes.'

'About those. Were you sleeping with the lead actress in real life?' Her imagination had run away with her during those scenes. Lying in Oliver's embrace, it was all too easy to imagine that she was watching him make love to her.

'She was engaged.'

'That doesn't change my question.'

'You don't think much of my acting.'

'On the contrary. Those kisses looked pretty authentic. I just wondered if you really are *that* good.'

'At kissing or acting?'

She noticed he still hadn't answered her original question but she was prepared to let it go for now. She had other things on her mind.

She wanted to know how it would feel to be kissed the way he'd kissed the heroine. She wanted to know what it would be like to be kissed by Oliver.

'Kissing,' she replied.

'Those kisses were nothing. It's just part of acting.'

'Is it true there are acting classes to teach people how to kiss?'

'Yes. But I'm not going to admit to having to learn how to kiss a girl properly.'

'So, you've never done one of those classes.'

'No. I've never needed to.'

She would bet he hadn't. She was sure he knew exactly what to do in the bedroom, exactly how to get a girl into bed with him and what to do with her when she got there. He would have had plenty of experience. All he'd have to do was look into her eyes and then smile. Say a few charming words. Kat knew that if she spent enough time with him and he kept up his charm offensive it would only be a matter of time before she succumbed. She was horny just watching him on screen, let alone having his arm around her, his thigh resting against hers. She could still feel his breath on her cheek, his fingers in her hair. Her heart was pounding and she wondered if he could hear it. Her hands were sweaty, her underwear damp.

'Don't confuse real life with acting. In a movie you have to think about everything except the act itself. That's scripted. In a movie you have to get the angles right. You don't want hands in the wrong places, noses getting in the way, too much tongue, too much saliva. It's *usually* all make-believe. And there are lots of different kisses.'

'What do you mean?'

'Think about the way you kiss your dad or your cousins and then think about the way you kissed your first boyfriend.'

She cringed at the thought. 'I'd rather not think about that.'

'Why not?'

'I was fifteen and it was a disaster.'

'Your second boyfriend, then.'

'That was a bit better.'

'How many boyfriends have you had?'

'A few. The choices are a bit limited out here, and you said it yourself—everyone is connected somehow. We all went to school together or are related.'

'I've learned that's not completely true. Plenty of people seem to have moved here from somewhere else. Surely there's an opportunity there. And what about when you were in Adelaide?'

'Yes, there were definitely more options then.' With the added bonus that they didn't have to be introduced to any of her over-protective family. But the only serious relationship she'd ever had had ended when she came back to Coober Pedy. She'd hoped he might follow her, but what was there here for him? She couldn't blame her ex for not wanting to live here. She had never intended to still be here at the age of twenty-seven. She had wanted to see the world but she felt duty bound to stay in Coober Pedy. She was waging a constant battle between her own desires and her beliefs as a daughter. 'What about you?'

'No boyfriends,' he smiled.

'Girlfriends?'

'Not as many as you might think. Now, where were we?' He reached towards her and ran his hand from her shoulder down her arm as he redirected the subject. Kat's skin tingled and her body sprang to life. He flipped her hand over and his thumb made slow circles over the sensitive skin of her wrist. She could scarcely remember her own name, let alone what they'd been talking about. 'We were talking about kisses, I think.'

Kat took a deep breath, closed her eyes

briefly and then forced herself to refocus as she opened them. 'What's next after the first kiss?'

'Technically, the second. But in reality, there are always more first kisses.'

'How do you figure that?'

'Every new person is a new kiss. Another first kiss.'

'Until you find *the* person,' she argued. 'The one you want to spend the rest of your life with.'

'Let's forget about numbering the kisses and just think about the way you want to kiss me.'

'I never said I wanted to kiss you.'

'Are you sure?' he teased and she nearly gave in. But she wanted him to make the first move. 'Anyway,' he said when she stayed silent, 'there are plenty more types of kisses.'

'Like what?'

'The kiss between two friends.'

He leant in close and kissed her on the cheek. His hands were on her elbows. The kiss was chaste.

The light from the movie screen played across his face, illuminating his eyes. He was looking at her closely and she was spell bound. He lifted his hand and ran his thumb across her cheek, stopping just in front of her ear.

His fingers slid under her hair, gently caress-ing her neck.

Her eyes were locked with his. Her lips parted.

He brought his face close to hers and said, 'And then there's this one.'

CHAPTER FIVE

HE PRESSED HIS lips close to her ear. She felt them on her earlobe as he ran his fingers down the back of her arm. The hairs on her arms were tingling. She'd never known the back of her arm could be an erogenous zone. Her whole body was tingling, desperate for his touch.

His other hand was behind her neck, his fingers splayed along the bones of her spine. His head dipped towards hers as her eyes drifted closed.

His lips pressed softly against hers.

She sighed and parted her lips on a breath.

Oliver's touch grew firmer and Kat opened her mouth further. His tongue was inside her, touching her, tasting her. He tasted like chocolate.

She melted into his embrace as the kiss deepened.

Their first kiss.

'I've wanted to do that since I first saw you,' he said when they finally came up for air.

'Was it worth waiting for?'

'You tell me.'

She nodded. It had been everything she'd hoped for. And more.

'Now do you believe me? My acting kisses are very different. That was me. All me. There's a big difference to kissing someone when you're surrounded by cameras, and when you're alone under the stars.'

'We're hardly alone.'

'You've been on set. You've seen how crowded it gets. This is as much privacy as I need when I'm kissing someone.'

'Can I have that one again?'

He shook his head. She was disappointed; it had been a pretty amazing kiss.

'We only get one first kiss,' he said. 'That's why it had to be perfect.'

'What comes next?'

'This one.'

He rolled her over, resting her back on the pile of pillows, trapping her under his weight. He pressed his lips to the side of her face, in front of her ear, before moving lower, dropping kisses along her jaw. His mouth moved lower still as he dropped feather-light kisses down her neck and along her collarbone.

He flicked the strap of her sundress off her shoulder and his fingers grazed her breast. Her nipple peaked as his lips pressed against the swell of her breast.

She put her index finger under his chin and lifted his head, bringing his lips back to hers. She slid her arms around his neck as she pressed herself against him.

His tongue explored her mouth. Tasting. Teasing, deeper and harder this time. There was an urgency to their movements now.

His mouth moved back to her jaw line, her neck. He pushed the fabric of her dress aside and cupped her breast with his hand as his thumb deliberately stroked across her nipple. He pushed the lace of her bra to one side, exposing her breast to the caress of his lips. He ran his tongue over her nipple and Kat dissolved.

She felt his hand trace over the curve of her hip, the thin cotton of her dress no protection against the heat of his hand. His mouth was still at her breast, his fingers were on her bare knee. Now his fingers were on the inside of her thigh.

Her skin was on fire. A waterfall of heat and desire started in her belly, overflowed and ran through her like a river.

His fingers moved higher until they came

to rest just below the junction of her thighs. It took all her willpower not to spread her legs for him and beg him not to stop. She needed to remember where they were. Who she was. But it was almost impossible. He was sending her crazy.

He seemed to sense just when enough was enough. His movements stilled, pausing right at the last moment, the moment before they wouldn't be able to rein in their desires.

Kat was panting. Dizzy. 'What was that one called?'

'That was called "Your place or mine?".' His lips were on her neck again. She could feel her pulse under the gentle caress of his mouth. He lifted his head and looked into her eyes. 'Would you like to come and spend the night with me?'

She wasn't surprised to find herself giving his suggestion serious consideration. She wasn't ready to say goodnight.

'I think my concussion still needs monitoring,' he added.

'You told me your headache had gone.'

He grinned. 'It has. I seem to have made a remarkable recovery.'

'Did you even have a headache?'

Oliver lifted his hands in surrender. 'I swear

I did. But it *has* gone, and it's fun to wind you up.'

'And you're all about fun, aren't you?'

'Yes. I am. That's not a crime. Fun can be very satisfying. You've had fun tonight, haven't you?'

She nodded.

'And the fun doesn't need to stop now. I've seen this movie.' Kat hadn't even noticed that the second feature had started. 'What do you say, shall we blow this joint?'

Kat didn't hesitate. She didn't think about her answer, she just went with her feelings. She knew her night wasn't over yet. She nodded again. Decision made.

'Are you sure?' Oliver checked. 'You promised George you'd stay away from me.'

She grinned. 'We both knew that was never going to happen.'

Her capitulation had not so much been a matter of time as a matter of timing. Of opportunity. And she knew this was her opportunity. She couldn't spend the whole night with him but they had a few more hours.

There was nothing that made her think this was a bad idea. Which wasn't to say it was a good idea. It probably wasn't one of her best, but there had been so many experiences she had missed out on in life because she worried about what other people might think.

She knew that never bothered Oliver. He had publicists and agents to worry for him.

There was no one here to see what she was up to.

There were so many reasons why this wasn't a great idea. They were complete opposites. She was all about family and helping people. He was about himself. He wasn't staying and she wasn't planning on leaving. But that was exactly why it could work. It could only ever be a fling. She was under no illusions that they could have a proper relationship and she assumed he was of the same opinion.

There were so many reasons why this wasn't a great idea but she didn't care. They were both consenting adults. No one was going to get hurt, she thought as she started the car and left the drive-in.

'Wow.' Kat collapsed onto the bed. Despite the fact that she was in Oliver's underground hotel room, where the temperature was a constant twenty-five degrees, a thin veil of sweat coated her body, testament to their energetic lovemaking.

'You can thank Lotte,' Oliver said.

'Lotte?'

'A German girl who took my virginity when I was fifteen and introduced me to the wonderful delights of women.'

'If I ever meet Lotte I will remember to thank her,' Kat smiled.

'You're not shocked that I was fifteen?'

Kat laughed. 'I might have only been having my first proper kiss, if you could call it that, at fifteen, but most of my friends skipped that bit. They went straight to getting married and having babies, sometimes not in that order. How old was Lotte?'

'Nineteen.'

'Now, *that's* a bit shocking. Is that even legal?'

'I have no idea. Possibly not. But I didn't care.' He shrugged and grinned. 'Show me a randy fifteen-year-old boy who is going to say no to a gorgeous, experienced older woman.'

'Where does a fifteen-year-old go to meet a nineteen-year-old Mata Hari?'

'My father was stationed in Germany at the time. I had one of my brother's IDs. We looked enough alike that the bars and clubs didn't really care. Isaac had just left home—Dad kicked him out when he announced he was gay. That really started my rebellious years. I was sick of following the rules. What did it get us? I realised it was always going to be my father's way or the highway, so I started exploring the highway. Sneaking off, lying. I couldn't wait to get out of home. I was miserable and I missed Isaac.'

'Where did he go?'

'He got a scholarship to university. He's an architect now. Living in Spain.'

'Do you see him very often?'

'Not often. Our lives are very different. He's married now, to his long-term partner.'

'Do you like his partner?'

'I do. But we don't have a lot in common any more. Our careers are different, our lifestyles too. I don't mean because he's gay, but he's very settled, nine-to-five work days, four weeks' holiday, vacations in Europe and Africa. He's happy.'

'And what about you? Are you happy?'

'I am now. Leaving home was the best thing I ever did. Our father was constantly disappointed in us. Nothing we did was ever good enough. I stopped trying to please him. Leaving home was the only way I was going to be able to find out who I was. And what about you? When are you going to leave home?'

'I went to Adelaide to study when I was eighteen but I came back when my mum died.'

'That was a while ago now; you said your friends are married with kids, but not you?

You've escaped all that? Or do you have an ex-husband hiding in a mine, waiting for the chance to hunt me down?'

'You've been in too many movies. I don't have an ex-husband. I want to find someone who will give me what my parents had. My parents were married for thirty-two years and they adored each other. I am looking for my soulmate.' She rolled onto her side and tucked her leg over Oliver's, craning her head to kiss him firmly on his mouth. 'And now I need to go.'

'You're not staying?'

She shook her head. 'My father will expect me home. He always leaves a light on and he'll look for my car in the morning. If he doesn't see it, he'll worry.'

'Why don't you call him?'

'And tell him what? That I'm staying out all night to have wild sex with a gorgeous man?'

'I'm flattered. But perhaps your father doesn't need to hear all the details.'

'You do remember what he does for a living?'

'So, it's not an ex-husband but a father I have to worry about.'

'Remember, he warned me against men like you.'

Oliver burst out laughing. 'Men like me? What does that even mean?'

'Charmers. Heartbreakers. Men who are only after one thing.'

'I told you, don't believe everything you read. I've dated a lot of women—it keeps me in the headlines and is good for my career—but I certainly haven't slept with them all. I will admit, though, that I am after you.'

'And now that you've had me, is that it?'

'No. Stay here and I'll prove it to you.' His fingers found her naked breast and he brushed lightly over her nipple, sending waves of desire through her.

She placed her hand over his and lifted it from her body before she capitulated. 'I can't, I have to go. I need to get some sleep.'

'You can sleep here in a minute,' he said as he lowered his head and took her nipple in his mouth.

Kat arched her back as his tongue circled her breast. She almost gave in. 'I have to go to work early tomorrow.' He sucked on her nipple as his hand slid from her waist over her hip. 'But why don't you come over for dinner tomorrow night?'

She hadn't intended to invite him but the invitation was out there now and she couldn't take it back. She would blame her hormones.

She couldn't think clearly while his mouth and hands worked their magic.

She wriggled out from underneath him and sat up. She needed to go before she said anything else she didn't really mean. Her mouth was working independently of her brain, or maybe her brain just wasn't working at all; maybe it was too overloaded by her other senses.

'I can't. We're filming tomorrow.'

'At night?'

Oliver wouldn't meet her eyes and she knew he wasn't telling her everything. She should just let it go. She should be relieved that he said no but she knew he was lying to her about something and she couldn't leave it alone.

'No,' he admitted.

'So, you have got what you wanted and now you'll walk away?'

'I'm not walking away but I don't do family.'

What the hell did that mean? She was desperate to know but she let it slide. She knew from his tone he wasn't going to discuss it further and she didn't need to know.

She bit her tongue as she got dressed. She didn't want to end the night on a fight. She didn't need to push the point. She shouldn't have invited him in the first place.

* * *

Oliver had been tempted to accept Kat's dinner invitation for this evening before common sense prevailed. Going on a few dates and fixing his reputation was one thing. Meeting her family was another thing altogether. It wasn't something he needed to do. It wasn't something he was prepared to do.

He was only in town for a few weeks, long enough to have some fun but not long enough for anything serious, and that suited him fine. Besides, he didn't have a great track record with families, his own included. And even if hers were wonderful, what would be the point of meeting them? He liked Kat but he wasn't going to get involved in her life. He knew he couldn't give her the things she wanted.

She'd told him she wanted to find her soulmate, and that wasn't him. He didn't believe in soulmates. His brother was the one exception. He though Isaac and his partner were a perfect match.

Oliver had never let himself fall in love. He'd had one relationship that he'd thought had the potential to become something serious but it had ended badly. His girlfriend had cheated on him, blamed him for not paying her enough attention. He knew he'd failed, he'd been focused on establishing his career, and he'd disappointed her.

He didn't want to be in a position again where he could disappoint someone, so he chose to keep his distance from people. He didn't date seriously and he didn't see his family. It was better not to get involved. That way people didn't develop expectations and he wouldn't disappoint.

His family was fractured.

He was a disappointment.

He avoided families for those very reasons.

But he couldn't get Kat out of his mind. He spent the afternoon filming a scene with Julia but it was Kat's face he was picturing. Her dark eyes, her smooth, lithe body. Her full red lips that did, amazingly, taste like summer cherries.

Jesus, he was hard again even now.

And, even though he knew he wouldn't go to dinner, it didn't stop him from thinking about Kat, from imagining what she was doing right at that moment, from thinking about what he was missing.

He knew that Kat's family had shaped her into the person she was. Into the compassionate, generous and open-hearted woman he was enjoying getting to know. He knew they were close and assumed they weren't as broken or as complicated as his own, but that still didn't mean he needed to meet them. He didn't want to risk disappointing Kat. Or her family. He knew he wasn't the man she was looking for. There was no need for him to meet her family.

It wasn't family he was missing. Kat's or his own. He was simply missing Kat.

Kat was glad she was rostered on to work; it gave her something to keep her mind occupied for the day. She might as well be at work, seeing as Oliver had blown her off. Being busy would stop her from thinking about him. Well, that had been her reasoning. She'd thought it would keep her busy but the shift had been quiet. Usually she was happy about that but today she needed the distraction. Just a minor vehicle accident or a suspected heart attack that turned out to be indigestion would have been enough. But she'd had far too much time on her hands and she spent it vacillating between reliving last night and wondering why Oliver wouldn't come to dinner. Was it really that he just didn't like being around other people's families, or did it mean he'd got what he wanted and she wouldn't see him again?

She'd been kidding herself to think they could have something meaningful. Family was everything to her and she couldn't imagine being with someone who didn't understand that.

She'd checked the filming schedule—Sunday was supposed to be a rest day—and she'd seen that nothing was listed. She hated that she was checking up on him but she couldn't stop herself. He'd said it was a closed set. Was it a love scene? Was he lying? Her thoughts went backwards and forwards...there were a thousand possibilities and she knew she could go crazy trying to work out what it all meant. Maybe it meant nothing.

She was relieved when the phone finally rang.

'Ambulance. What's your emergency?'

'I've got a fifty-eight-year-old man with severe stomach pains.'

'Oliver? Is that you?' she asked before her initial excitement at hearing his voice gave way to the realisation that he'd called 000, not her specifically.

'Kat? Yes, it's me. I'm with George. He's in a lot of pain and I don't know what to do.'

'Where is his pain?'

'Right side. Under his ribs. Could he be having a heart attack?'

'Tell me what other symptoms he has,' she said, trying to keep him calm. 'Any shortness emergency surgery but it should be done some time in the next three days. The flying doctor will transfer him if necessary.'

of breath?' She could hear Oliver relaying her questions to George.

'No,' came the reply.

'Oliver, can you put the phone on speaker? George can hear my questions—he'll only have to nod yes or no and you can then pass the information on to me.' She paused briefly and then continued, 'Chest pain?'

'Yes,' came Oliver's reply.

'Back pain?'

'No.'

'Arm pain?'

'No.'

'Has he vomited?'

'Yes.'

'But he's not having difficulty breathing?'

'No.'

Kat scribbled a note to Dave while she spoke to Oliver.

Chest pain?
Abdominal pain?

Dave began a quick check of their supplies before lifting the keys for the ambulance off their hook.

'I don't think I can get him in the car to take him to the hospital,' Oliver told her.

'It's all right. We'll come to you. Where are you?'

'Still on set. We're in George's trailer.'

Kat was mollified. Oliver hadn't been lying to her about having to work. 'We're on the way.'

Kat and Dave arrived on set to find a restless George; he was unable to find a comfortable position.

The air-conditioning was working overtime but he still felt hot to the touch. Kat took his temperature and observed his colour. He had a tinge of yellow about him.

Kat removed the thermometer from his ear and relayed the elevated reading to Dave. She lifted George's shirt to palpate his stomach.

'Where is the pain?'

George indicated his right side.

'When did the pain start?'

'After lunch, maybe a couple of hours ago,' he said.

There was a small, faded scar in the right lower quadrant. 'Have you had your appendix removed?' Kat asked.

George nodded as Kat continued to feel his abdomen.

Dave was busy attaching ECG leads to George's chest. Kat clipped an oximeter onto his finger and listened to his respiration rate.

His oxygen saturation was slightly low, heart rate was elevated, respiration rate rapid, temperature high, but the ECG trace was normal.

'Take a deep breath for me, George,' Kat instructed as she pushed her fingers into the upper right quadrant of his abdomen. George gasped with pain, holding his breath until Kat released the pressure on his gallbladder.

'OK, George, good news—it's not a heart attack and it's not appendicitis.'

'What's the bad news?' Oliver asked.

'I think it's probably a blocked bile duct.'

'What causes that?'

'Gallstones. I'm not surprised you're feeling terrible, George—it is a very painful condition, but easily remedied. You'll need further testing though.'

'Here?' Oliver asked.

Dave drew up a dose of analgesia to s~~ ~~ controlling George's pain.

'No,' Kat replied. 'We'll take him ~~ ~~ hospital for pain relief but he'll need ~~ ~~ Port Augusta or Adelaide for furthe~~ ~~

'And then what?'

'If it's gallstones he'll probab~~ ~~ gery.' Kat was almost certain ~~ ~~ nosis was correct and with ac~~ ~~ surgery was almost always re~~ ~~

CHAPTER SIX

KAT EMERGED FROM the water and Oliver's brain froze. Droplets of water clung to her body and her skin glistened. She wore a black bikini; he'd seen a thousand different women wearing black bikinis before—he had a house on Malibu Beach and gorgeous women were everywhere—but none of them had affected him the way Kat did.

He couldn't believe she'd accepted his invitation to come to Adelaide with him.

George had been transferred to Adelaide for surgery, so filming had been put on hold, giving Oliver, and the rest of the cast and crew, a few days off. Oliver had offered to fly down to Adelaide as well. George didn't need him—he had his assistant, Erica—but Oliver used it as an excuse to invite Kat to go too. And here she was.

They would have at least three days in the city. Three days that had the potential to be so much better than any date he had imagined. He'd booked them into the only five-star hotel at Glenelg Beach and as he watched the sway of her hips as she came towards him he wondered about his chances of getting her back to their suite and ravishing her before dinner.

No, he'd show her that there was more to him than the persona that the tabloids loved to write about. His womanising ways were, as he'd told her, mostly fabricated for publicity and he wasn't searching for publicity today. He had a corporate credit card and he'd used his alias when he'd booked the hotel room. The next couple of days were about him and Kat. He hadn't asked what she'd told her father—he didn't care; it wasn't any of his business.

Her olive skin was tanned and golden and Oliver feasted his eyes on her as she came out of the ocean. Her dark hair was slick and wet and he watched as she lifted her arms and gathered her hair in one handful and squeezed the salt water from it. Her breasts rose with the movement, two perfect golden orbs, and Oliver struggled to keep his eyes up.

Jesus, she made him feel like a horny teenager. He was in a constant state of arousal when she was near him, and her being almost naked was not helping. He couldn't remember the last time a woman had driven him to distraction the way Kat did and it made it difficult to remember that he was trying to be on his best behaviour. But try he would.

He couldn't, however, resist just one kiss.

He stepped towards her and met her in the shallows. He slid his arm around her waist. Her skin was damp and cool and smooth. He bent his head and kissed her.

He needed to keep it brief; he was only wearing a pair of swim shorts—there wasn't much to keep him decent.

'Are you worried someone will see you?' she asked as his lips left hers.

He noticed she didn't say 'us' and he knew she was thinking of him being stalked by the paparazzi, but he really didn't care. Not today. Not now.

'No one knows we're here,' he told her, including her with him. 'No one is expecting to see me.' He was wearing a baseball cap, more out of habit than for a disguise, but it had the added advantage that it shaded his eyes. He knew they were his most identifying feature. He had booked into the hotel under an alias and as far as he knew no one had been tipped off. He supposed the airline staff could have said something if they'd recognised him, but their plane tickets had been booked using the same corporate card and the plane had been tiny—twenty seats at most—and no one knew where they were headed once it had landed in Adelaide. He was confident they could go undetected. He had to admit, while he courted the paparazzi in LA, as it was important to keep them on side, it was refreshing to be incognito. It was a novelty to be able to pretend he had a normal life even if he suspected he'd grow tired and bored of normal after a while. But, for the moment, if it meant he could hold Kat in his arms on a public beach and be left alone he was all for that.

He kissed her again for good measure before taking her hand. He picked up one of their towels from the warm sand and wrapped it around her shoulders, hugging her close as he dried her back. The sun was low over the horizon now, turning the sky pink and gold, and he had plans to sip champagne on their balcony as they watched it set.

He took her hand and walked along the beach, leaving footprints in the soft sand by the water's edge. The tide was on its way out, the moats around the sandcastles were emptying and the beach was starting to empty too as families thought about getting home to feed their kids. There was still a group of teenagers jumping off the jetty into the sea. They stopped temporarily if the lifeguards or police of breath?' She could hear Oliver relaying her questions to George.

'No,' came the reply.

'Oliver, can you put the phone on speaker? George can hear my questions—he'll only have to nod yes or no and you can then pass the information on to me.' She paused briefly and then continued, 'Chest pain?'

'Yes,' came Oliver's reply.

'Back pain?'

'No.'

'Arm pain?'

'No.'

'Has he vomited?'

'Yes.'

'But he's not having difficulty breathing?'

'No.'

Kat scribbled a note to Dave while she spoke to Oliver.

Chest pain?
Abdominal pain?

Dave began a quick check of their supplies before lifting the keys for the ambulance off their hook.

'I don't think I can get him in the car to take him to the hospital,' Oliver told her.

'It's all right. We'll come to you. Where are you?'

'Still on set. We're in George's trailer.'

Kat was mollified. Oliver hadn't been lying to her about having to work. 'We're on the way.'

Kat and Dave arrived on set to find a restless George; he was unable to find a comfortable position.

The air-conditioning was working overtime but he still felt hot to the touch. Kat took his temperature and observed his colour. He had a tinge of yellow about him.

Kat removed the thermometer from his ear and relayed the elevated reading to Dave. She lifted George's shirt to palpate his stomach.

'Where is the pain?'

George indicated his right side.

'When did the pain start?'

'After lunch, maybe a couple of hours ago,' he said.

There was a small, faded scar in the right lower quadrant. 'Have you had your appendix removed?' Kat asked.

George nodded as Kat continued to feel his abdomen.

Dave was busy attaching ECG leads to George's chest. Kat clipped an oximeter onto his finger and listened to his respiration rate.

His oxygen saturation was slightly low, heart rate was elevated, respiration rate rapid, temperature high, but the ECG trace was normal.

'Take a deep breath for me, George,' Kat instructed as she pushed her fingers into the upper right quadrant of his abdomen. George gasped with pain, holding his breath until Kat released the pressure on his gallbladder.

'OK, George, good news—it's not a heart attack and it's not appendicitis.'

'What's the bad news?' Oliver asked.

'I think it's probably a blocked bile duct.'

'What causes that?'

'Gallstones. I'm not surprised you're feeling terrible, George—it is a very painful condition, but easily remedied. You'll need further testing though.'

'Here?' Oliver asked.

Dave drew up a dose of analgesia to start controlling George's pain.

'No,' Kat replied. 'We'll take him to the hospital for pain relief but he'll need to go to Port Augusta or Adelaide for further tests.'

'And then what?'

'If it's gallstones he'll probably need surgery.' Kat was almost certain that her diagnosis was correct and with acute cholecystitis surgery was almost always required. 'It's not emergency surgery but it should be done some time in the next three days. The flying doctor will transfer him if necessary.'

CHAPTER SIX

KAT EMERGED FROM the water and Oliver's brain froze. Droplets of water clung to her body and her skin glistened. She wore a black bikini; he'd seen a thousand different women wearing black bikinis before—he had a house on Malibu Beach and gorgeous women were everywhere—but none of them had affected him the way Kat did.

He couldn't believe she'd accepted his invitation to come to Adelaide with him.

George had been transferred to Adelaide for surgery, so filming had been put on hold, giving Oliver, and the rest of the cast and crew, a few days off. Oliver had offered to fly down to Adelaide as well. George didn't need him—he had his assistant, Erica—but Oliver used it as an excuse to invite Kat to go too. And here she was.

They would have at least three days in the city. Three days that had the potential to be so much better than any date he had imagined. He'd booked them into the only five-star hotel at Glenelg Beach and as he watched the sway of her hips as she came towards him he wondered about his chances of getting her back to their suite and ravishing her before dinner.

No, he'd show her that there was more to him than the persona that the tabloids loved to write about. His womanising ways were, as he'd told her, mostly fabricated for publicity and he wasn't searching for publicity today. He had a corporate credit card and he'd used his alias when he'd booked the hotel room. The next couple of days were about him and Kat. He hadn't asked what she'd told her father—he didn't care; it wasn't any of his business.

Her olive skin was tanned and golden and Oliver feasted his eyes on her as she came out of the ocean. Her dark hair was slick and wet and he watched as she lifted her arms and gathered her hair in one handful and squeezed the salt water from it. Her breasts rose with the movement, two perfect golden orbs, and Oliver struggled to keep his eyes up.

Jesus, she made him feel like a horny teenager. He was in a constant state of arousal when she was near him, and her being almost naked was not helping. He couldn't remember the last time a woman had driven him to distraction the way Kat did and it made it difficult to remember that he was trying to be on his best behaviour. But try he would.

He couldn't, however, resist just one kiss.

He stepped towards her and met her in the shallows. He slid his arm around her waist. Her skin was damp and cool and smooth. He bent his head and kissed her.

He needed to keep it brief; he was only wearing a pair of swim shorts—there wasn't much to keep him decent.

'Are you worried someone will see you?' she asked as his lips left hers.

He noticed she didn't say 'us' and he knew she was thinking of him being stalked by the paparazzi, but he really didn't care. Not today. Not now.

'No one knows we're here,' he told her, including her with him. 'No one is expecting to see me.' He was wearing a baseball cap, more out of habit than for a disguise, but it had the added advantage that it shaded his eyes. He knew they were his most identifying feature. He had booked into the hotel under an alias and as far as he knew no one had been tipped off. He supposed the airline staff could have said something if they'd recognised him, but their plane tickets had been booked using the same corporate card and the plane had been tiny—twenty seats at most—and no one knew where they were headed once it had landed in Adelaide. He was confident they could go undetected. He had to admit, while he courted the paparazzi in LA, as it was important to keep them on side, it was refreshing to be incognito. It was a novelty to be able to pretend he had a normal life even if he suspected he'd grow tired and bored of normal after a while. But, for the moment, if it meant he could hold Kat in his arms on a public beach and be left alone he was all for that.

He kissed her again for good measure before taking her hand. He picked up one of their towels from the warm sand and wrapped it around her shoulders, hugging her close as he dried her back. The sun was low over the horizon now, turning the sky pink and gold, and he had plans to sip champagne on their balcony as they watched it set.

He took her hand and walked along the beach, leaving footprints in the soft sand by the water's edge. The tide was on its way out, the moats around the sandcastles were emptying and the beach was starting to empty too as families thought about getting home to feed their kids. There was still a group of teenagers jumping off the jetty into the sea. They stopped temporarily if the lifeguards or police turned up before they were at it again. Oliver thought it looked like fun and it was exactly the sort of thing he would have done in his youth too, but he didn't tell Kat that. He knew she liked to abide by the rules.

They walked into the shade underneath the jetty and as they emerged from the other side he heard a woman screaming. Her English was heavily accented and her distress was making her hard to understand, but when he looked in the direction she was pointing, into the distance, into the waves, out past a rocky outcrop, he thought he could see a head bobbing in the water and being taken out to sea with the outgoing tide.

The lifeguard station was empty, unmanned at this time of day, although the surf lifesaving club was still open. But, even so, he and Kat were the closest people.

Oliver didn't hesitate. He knocked his baseball cap from his head, let go of Kat's hand and ran into the shallows, ignoring Kat's cry of, 'What are you doing?'

He splashed through the water until it was knee-deep and running became difficult. He dived into the sea and struck out around the rocks. He was a strong swimmer. He was used to the Pacific Ocean and, in comparison, the calm waters of the gulf didn't look too difficult, although he knew it was one thing to swim in calm waters and another to try to rescue a frightened, drowning man. Maybe he should have waited for the lifeguards but that extra minute or two could be the difference between a good outcome and a bad; between life and death.

He was getting closer. He saw the man's head disappear under the water. Oliver put his head down and kicked harder, willing himself to reach the man before it was too late.

The man was sinking.

Oliver dived down, searching underwater for the man.

He found him. He was fully clothed and wearing shoes. His eyes were closed.

Oliver came up behind him and got an arm around his chest. He was a dead weight as Oliver kicked to the surface. He hoped the man was only unconscious—surely he couldn't have drowned that quickly?

He knew he had to keep the man on his back, facing away from him, in order to keep control of the situation. If he regained consciousness and panicked, he'd most likely drag them both under.

It seemed to take for ever to reach the surface, and Oliver was breathing heavily as he broke through the waves. It was hard work. He fitted his fingers around the man's chin, keeping his head above water as he kicked in a side-stroke action and headed for the shore, recalling the lessons learned a lifetime ago in his summer swimming lessons as a schoolboy.

Two lifeguards appeared beside him on a board. One took the unconscious man from Oliver and dragged him onto his belly across the board.

'He's not breathing,' Oliver panted.

'Do you need a hand?' The second lifeguard held out a hand to Oliver as the first began paddling back to the beach. They were only fifty metres from the sand. Oliver was tired but now that he wasn't towing a ninety-kilogram dead weight he knew he'd make it. 'I'm OK, thanks,' he said. His pride wouldn't let him be rescued. 'I can swim in.'

His feet hit the sand and he stood, aware that his legs were shaky with fatigue and adrenalin, but he knew he'd be fine as long as he kept moving.

Kat was waiting on the shore. He wrapped one arm around her shoulders, careful not to lean on her, even though it was tempting.

The lifeguards had started performing CPR

on the rescued man and he could tell Kat was itching to help, but it wasn't her beat.

As they reached the lifeguards the man's chest started to move. The lifeguards quickly rolled him into the recovery position as he retched, sea water gushing from his mouth.

Bystanders had gathered, hovering around as the lifeguards called for an ambulance. Oliver was always amazed by people's curious fascination with disaster. He understood being curious—as an actor he'd made a habit of people-watching—but sticky-beaking at a potential tragedy was a whole different level in his opinion.

The lifeguards came over and thanked him for his assistance, even though he was sure some of them would have liked to berate him for diving in without thinking.

'You look like that actor,' said one.

'Oliver Harding,' said another.

'I get that a lot,' Oliver replied, not giving anything away. 'Name's Frank.' He stuck out his hand and shook theirs.

'Well, we appreciate your help, mate.'

'No worries,' he replied in his best Australian accent.

He could feel Kat looking sideways at him. She handed him his baseball cap and said, 'We need to get going, *Frank*.'

* * *

She waited until they were out of earshot from all the bystanders before she stopped walking and turned to Oliver.

'What was that all about?'

To his credit he didn't pretend not to know what she was asking. 'Frank is one of my aliases.'

'One of?' She raised an eyebrow. 'Is Oliver your real name?'

'Yes. Oliver James Harding, at your service,' he said with a mock bow.

'And when did you start speaking in an Aussie accent?'

'That's my job. Most of the movie crew are Aussies, and I've been paying attention on set. It's the best way to make people believe I am just a doppelgänger.'

'Why do you need a fake name?'

'I usually use it for checking into hotels, restaurants, that sort of thing. I don't expect special treatment, so I don't need to broadcast my movements. There's no need to give everyone a heads up about where I'm going to be and when. The paparazzi pay people to divulge that sort of information. If I want them to know my whereabouts there are ways of getting that information out to them, but if I want some privacy I need some measures to protect it. Mostly I'm happy to sign autographs or pose for photos, but I didn't think the lifeguards needed to deal with that palaver as well. I'm not saying that all of those bystanders would have wanted selfies or whatever, but in my experience at least some of them would and that can become a bit of a circus. It wasn't necessary and, besides, for the next couple of days I want it to just be us.'

She was more than happy for it to be just the two of them as well. She found it liberating being able to walk down the street and hold Oliver's hand and not worry about what people might say or think. If she found it liberating, she could just imagine how Oliver must feel. He was used to his every move being scrutinised and potentially splashed across the cover of a magazine, so she could understand the appeal of hiding his true identity.

They reached the hotel and Kat stepped inside as the doorman held the door. She felt as though she should apologise as they left sandy footprints on the spotless tiled floor. She smiled to herself as she wondered what the staff in this five-star hotel thought. She wondered if they could tell that she wasn't used to this level of luxury and attention. That she had never before stayed in a five-star, or even a four-star, hotel, had never been picked up from the airport by a chauffeur, had never slept with a Hollywood star.

'What name did you use to book the hotel?' She wondered if the hotel staff knew who he was.

'The same alias—Frank Foster.'

'How do you come up with the names? Is there a list somewhere of the top ten aliases?'

Oliver laughed. 'No. It was the name of one of my characters, one of my favourite parts.'

'That was the character in the movie we saw at the drive-in!'

'It was,' he said as he swiped the room card and held the door for her as she entered the penthouse suite. 'Would you like first shower before dinner?'

She smiled and reached one hand behind her back. She was looking forward to the next few days, and nights, in Adelaide. She was looking forward to spending time with Oliver, just the two of them without interruptions, with no work, no family. She hadn't hesitated when he'd asked her to come with him; she had three rostered days off and she was eager to spend more time exploring their attraction. One night in Coober Pedy hadn't been enough and she was prepared to forget that he 'didn't do family'. If he was keen to spend time with her alone she was happy with that.

Her fingers found the tie for her bikini top. 'I thought we could share,' she said as she tugged at the string. His mouth fell open as her top fell to the floor. She walked away from him but he caught up to her before she reached the bathroom. She stretched one hand out and turned the tap for the shower. He stretched one arm out and put his hand on her waist. He slid it up her belly until he was cupping her breast.

She turned towards him and pulled him under the water.

'What do you fancy for dinner?' Kat asked.

She was wrapped in the thick towelling robe from the hotel and he knew she was naked underneath. They'd only just stepped out of the shower but he debated about ordering Room Service and staying in. But he'd promised himself he would take her out and show her some fun. They'd be back in their room soon enough.

'Your choice,' he said. He couldn't care less what they ate. He wasn't thinking about food.

'I usually choose seafood when I come to the city. Fresh seafood isn't something we get a lot of in Coober Pedy.' She slipped the robe off as she walked into the walk-in wardrobe and Oliver wondered if it was too soon to take her to bed again.

No. He could wait. Sometimes letting the anticipation build was worth it. 'Can you guarantee me that no one will choke on a fish bone?'

'What do you mean?' She emerged from the wardrobe carrying a pair of high heels and dressed in a simple black halter-neck dress that highlighted her shoulders.

'We keep running into people who need saving. I need a rest from all that. No more blocked bile ducts, drowning men or pulling men out of mine shafts. In fact, we should just steer clear of all men for the next two days.'

Kat laughed as she sat on the edge of the bed and slipped her sandals on. She lifted one foot and rested it on her opposite knee, sliding her sandal on and fastening the strap around her slender ankle. Her dress rode up to reveal the inside of her thigh. Her legs were long and smooth and tanned. He never knew watching a woman get dressed could be as sexy as watching one undress.

'We need to visit George tomorrow.'

Oliver swallowed and tried to focus on what she was saying as he reminded himself to behave. He didn't want her to think that sex was all he had on his mind and that he wasn't interested in spending time with her if she had her clothes on. 'OK, apart from George. No more emergencies, just us.'

'OK.'

Kat stood and leant towards the mirror that hung over the dressing table beside the bed. Her dress clung to her hips as she bent forwards. Oliver's gaze travelled up, over the curve of her buttocks. He watched as she applied her red lipstick and it took all of his self-control to let her finish, take her hand and lead her out of their suite.

He held her hand as they walked along Jetty Road. A signboard outside a hotel caught his eye. 'What about here? They have karaoke.'

'Karaoke? I thought we were looking for somewhere to eat?'

'We can do both.'

'I don't think karaoke places are renowned for their food,' Kat said.

Oliver pointed to an announcement painted on the pub window. 'It says they won "Best Pub Restaurant" last year.'

'You really want to go to a karaoke restaurant? I thought you said you couldn't sing.'

'I said I wished I was a better singer. And I never said I intended to sing tonight.'

'Well, I certainly won't be singing,' Kat laughed.

'Let's have a look at the menu and then decide. It'll be fun.'

She knew he was all about fun and, looking at his expression, she didn't think she could refuse him. 'OK,' she said as he held the door for her and they stepped inside.

'Have a seat,' he said as he pulled a chair out for her, 'and I'll get some menus.'

He returned with menus, a glass of wine for her and a beer for him. 'Is wine OK? I can get you something else if you prefer?'

'This is fine, thanks.'

'What do you think?' Oliver asked as she perused the menu.

The pub looked newly refurbished, the crowd was well-dressed and the menu looked good. Kat watched as a waitress delivered plates of food to an adjacent table. 'The food looks good,' she admitted, 'I think I can maybe overlook the fact that I'll have to listen to some karaoke.'

Oliver smiled. She could overlook anything at all if she got to sit opposite him for the evening, she decided.

'Where did you learn to swim?' she asked after they had ordered. He had been amazing today, jumping in without hesitation to rescue that man.

'I live on the beach in LA. At Malibu. The

swell today was nothing compared to the Pacific Ocean. I've always lived near water. I was born in Italy, lived in Turkey, Hawaii and Germany. All the army bases had swimming pools and we spent summer holidays around the Mediterranean. I spent a lot of my spare time in the water. What about you?'

'I can swim but there's no way I'd be confident enough to jump in like you did. You've seen where I grew up. The town has a pool, and you've seen the lake, but I'm not used to waves. I didn't go out of my depth in the sea today.'

'Can I ask you something? The lifeguards revived the man, so why did he have to go off to hospital?'

'There is a latent risk after people take water into their lungs,' Kat explained. 'There's something called post-immersion syndrome, where your throat can spasm due to irritation of the vocal cords, which makes breathing difficult—that's more common in children—and there's also secondary drowning. If water gets into the lungs it can irritate them and cause pulmonary oedema, which is a build-up of fluid in the tiny air sacs that makes breathing difficult. He needs to be monitored, especially given his lack of English. The hospital will organise an interpreter to explain the risks and he may be discharged if they think he and his girlfriend understand what to watch for.'

'Will he be OK?'

'I would think so. He survived the drowning, and deaths from secondary drownings are extremely rare. At worst he might be unwell.' Kat reached across the table and held Oliver's hand. 'You saved his life.'

'A good day, then.'

'A very good day,' she said with a smile.

The karaoke began as they were finishing their meal, making conversation more difficult. Some of the singers were good, some were woeful, but because there was a prize at the end of the night there were plenty of participants. The winner would be decided by an audience vote.

'Some of these people should definitely save their singing for the shower,' Kat commented.

'You sure you don't want to have a go?'

'I'm positive,' she laughed.

'Can you excuse me?' Oliver said. 'I need to use the bathroom. Will you be all right on your own for a minute?'

'Of course, I'll be fine.' She loved the attention he paid her.

There was a scattered round of applause as another singer finished their song.

'And now, one final karaoke contestant. Give it up for… Frank!'

Kat looked at the stage. Was the MC introducing Oliver? He hadn't returned to their table yet but the stage was empty.

Then she heard a voice through the speakers. A male voice. Unaccompanied.

There was still no one on stage but he obviously had a microphone and, whoever it was, he could sing.

Kat looked around the bar.

Oliver was walking towards her. His blue eyes pinned her to the seat and the spotlight followed him as he sang.

A second spotlight fell on Kat and she hurriedly hid her face behind her hands as Oliver continued to sing about how he couldn't keep his eyes off her. She could feel herself blushing, and part of her wanted to slide under the table, but another part of her couldn't look away. She peeked through her fingers in time to see Oliver stop just before he reached her and step up onto the stage. He was poised and confident.

The music started up in accompaniment, just loud enough to be heard but still letting Oliver's voice shine. Kat was mesmerised. Oliver was born to be on stage.

The second spotlight dimmed, putting her back into the shadows.

The focus was all on Oliver. He didn't seem to mind. Kat knew he loved an audience but she also knew he was singing to her.

The crowd had fallen silent as soon as he'd started singing. They were expecting something special, nothing had been anywhere near as good as what they were hearing now.

He reached the chorus and invited everyone in the restaurant to sing with him. They didn't need to be asked twice. They didn't need to know the words; it was a simple repeat.

Oliver jumped down from the stage and offered his hand to Kat as the audience sang and clapped.

She knew he wanted to get her out of her seat but she hesitated for a fraction of a second, reluctant to dance in front of strangers. She was so used to worrying about what people would think, but then she realised that no one here knew her and no one would care about what she did—they were all too focused on Oliver.

He had the room eating out of his hand as he performed, so she could probably do naked cartwheels across the stage and still no one would give her a second glance.

She let him pull her to her feet.

He twirled her around, spinning her out and away from him as the crowd accompanied them vocally before pulling her in close, her back tucked into his side as he sang the next verse. She swayed with him as they moved in time to the music, oblivious now to the audience.

Thunderous applause surrounded them as he kissed her at the end of the song and returned her to her seat. He took a bow before he was unanimously declared the winner.

He graciously accepted his prize before quickly settling their tab so they could sneak away.

'Well, I don't know about you but that Frank Foster sure can sing,' Kat laughed as Oliver took her hand as they walked back to the hotel.

'Did you have fun?'

'I did.' It was the most fun she'd had in a long time; perhaps she should care less about what people might think and just let her hair down more often.

Kat felt as if she were floating. She was relaxed, sexually satisfied. Happy.

She and Oliver had gone for an early-morning swim, followed by a room service breakfast, followed by more lovemaking, and then they'd wandered through the shops. She was carrying several shopping bags, filled with clothes that would probably never see the light of day in Coober Pedy but which Oliver had insisted on buying for her as well as some gifts for her family.

'I could use a drink after that retail therapy,' Oliver said as he offloaded their purchases to the concierge. 'Would you like to grab a drink in the bar or…?' He paused, his train of thought interrupted, his attention caught by something else.

Kat turned and saw a woman walking towards them. She was short, blonde, extremely thin and expertly put together. Her hair, make-up and clothing were all immaculate. She looked just the type of person who would be in the lobby of a five-star hotel, and Kat's curiosity was piqued.

'Philippa! What are you doing here?' Oliver greeted her.

The woman looked over at Kat, not trying to hide her curiosity. 'Who is this?' she asked as she looked Kat up and down.

Kat frowned. She was wondering the same thing.

'This is Kat Angelis; she's an emergency paramedic, and she's overseeing my stunt work.'

'You're not working right now, though.

George is in hospital,' the woman stated, clearly implying that she thought Kat shouldn't be there.

'Kat, this is Philippa Corcoran, my publicist.' Oliver introduced her, choosing to ignore the woman's implication.

Philippa nodded in Kat's direction before turning back to Oliver. 'I need to speak to you, Oliver. In private.'

Kat waited for Oliver to tell her that this wasn't a good time, but Philippa hadn't finished.

'We have a problem,' she added before Oliver could speak.

CHAPTER SEVEN

PHILIPPA WAS BEING rude and Oliver thought about arguing, but something in Philippa's demeanour stopped him from dismissing his publicist.

'How did you find me?'

'You checked in with your credit card. I see the statements.'

She had tracked him down and then flown halfway across the world to see him. Her news must be bad. Too bad for her to deliver over the phone, and he didn't want her to tell him what it was in front of Kat. Who knew what Philippa had to say? He didn't want Kat to hear anything sordid about him. Not without his knowing first what was going on.

'I'm really sorry, Kat, but could you give us a minute?'

'I'll get a coffee in the lounge,' she said.

He could tell from her expression that she

wasn't happy, but she didn't argue. He'd make it up to her later.

Kat headed for the lounge and Oliver swiped his card and called the lift for the penthouse suite.

The penthouse door had scarcely closed behind them before Philippa pulled a folder out of her designer bag and handed it to Oliver.

He took it reluctantly. 'What is this?'

'You're being sued.'

'Sued? By whom?'

'The parents of Natalie Hanson, the girl who overdosed at your house.'

'What? That's ridiculous. I wasn't even there.'

'Unfortunately that doesn't matter. She died on your property.'

'And that gives them grounds to sue me?' Oliver stood in the middle of the living room and rifled through the folder. There was a legal document, he assumed the lawsuit, and photos of a young girl. He knew it was Natalie. She was beautiful, happy, smiling, looking as if she didn't have a care in the world. He felt for her parents, they didn't deserve this, but that didn't make it his fault.

Philippa took a seat on the sofa. 'They're saying you had a duty of care. They're saying their daughter didn't have a drug problem. That she must have got the drugs at your house.'

'The police thought she brought the drugs with her,' he said as he dropped the folder onto the coffee table.

'They haven't been able to prove that. There's a copy of the police report in that file.'

'Well, I definitely didn't supply them!' This could ruin his reputation. He'd been working hard to clean up his image, but stories about the number of celebrities he'd dated would seem trivial in comparison to an alleged drug problem. 'In all the thousands of stories I've had printed about me there's never been anything to suggest I'm into illegal drugs.'

'I know that,' Philippa said calmly. 'I know most of what they print about you isn't true, but you know the saying—throw enough mud and some of it will stick. We've worked hard to get you back in the good books, to keep you employed. The movie studios are jumpy. They don't want bad publicity. We need to manage this.'

Oliver sank into a chair. He didn't care what people thought about him but he did care about his career. 'How bad is it?' he asked.

'They're not suing you as a dealer. They're suing you as the landlord. Their argument is that you are liable because it's your property. We need to make sure your name is cleared.'

He had been sent to Australia to make a film in the middle of nowhere as a way of supposedly keeping him out of trouble, but that plan obviously hadn't worked and he knew this lawsuit could be a big problem.

How was he going to explain this to Kat? He really didn't want her to think trouble followed him. Thank God she'd agreed to give him and Philippa some privacy. He hated to think of her hearing this.

Philippa was talking and he forced his mind off Kat and back to what she was saying.

'This is serious. I've spoken to your lawyers already but we need to do some damage control and we also need some positive publicity to counteract any negative stories that come your way.'

'What do you suggest?' He couldn't think straight. All he could think about was Kat's reaction. She was so black and white; she thrived on following the rules. What would she make of this latest scandal? What would she think of him?

'I think you should get engaged.'

'What?'

'You need to show that you've reformed your partying, playboy ways. I know you don't have a drug-taking history, but drugs and partying are a marriage made in heaven for the media, and it only takes a few tabloids to make some suggestions and you have an even bigger PR problem.'

'But that playboy persona was just an image. You know that's not really me. You helped create it!'

'Again, *I* know that, but it's an image you've—we've—spent years selling. Now it's about how we manage it. An engagement is a perfect solution. You need a fiancée, someone who will stand by you and support you while you sort out these allegations. It will give you some positive publicity.'

'And who will agree to be a fake fiancée? Where do you suggest I find someone to play that role?'

Philippa didn't miss a beat.

'Someone trustworthy,' she said. 'An actress. We need someone who is wholesome, which will give you credibility. Someone the public can trust. A fan favourite. Someone they will believe is with you for all the right reasons and therefore you couldn't possibly have done the things you've been accused of because otherwise how would you have got her to fall in love with you?' She reached into her bag and pulled a stack of glossy A4 pages from it. Each page had a photo on it and Oliver could see they were actor bios. She handed him the sheaf of photos. 'I have a short list of actresses who I think would be perfect. I'm pleased you're out of America. That will work in our favour. We'll get you back to Coober Pedy asap, where the paparazzi and the media can't find you. You choose someone from those bios and I will organise a media announcement. I will control it all.'

'Is that why you're here, in person?'

Knowing that he, once again, needed someone to clean up his image was upsetting. Particularly as he was in this situation through no fault of his own.

Philippa was nodding. 'I needed to find you and speak to you before the paparazzi did. I needed you to see that my idea makes sense.'

'No.' Oliver threw the pile of photos onto the table. 'None of this makes sense. It's ridiculous. I had nothing to do with that girl's death and I will fight the lawsuit. Why do I have to create fake news about myself? I thought we were trying to clean up my reputation; I thought part of that was to stay out of the media spotlight. Isn't that one of the reasons I'm down under?'

'Yes. But the story is already out. Natalie's parents have gone to the media. We have to do something. We really do need to counter-attack with something positive. We can't have the media linking your name to a lawsuit and a lawsuit only. We need to give them something else, something good. I think it's our, *your*, best option.'

'I'm not interested.'

'I think you should consider it. Maybe read the stories that have been printed so far. You might agree you don't really have much choice.'

Philippa passed him a third stack of paper, this time printed copies of tabloid magazine articles. He took a cursory glance—he didn't need more than that to see they were all saying the same thing—this actress had died in his house. His name was being linked by association and her parents were suing him. It didn't matter that the tabloids weren't actually mentioning that he hadn't been in the house, that he'd been on location, filming. Fans would put two and two together and get whatever the hell number they pleased; he knew how this business worked. A few photos, a few quotes taken out of context, a few interviews with 'close friends' and there was a story. Suddenly he was into illegal drugs and a girl had died because of it. It was all that was needed to sell the magazines.

'Think of it as a job,' Philippa said. 'A role. You can play the part of the law-abiding, con-scientious, clean-living, loved-up fiancé.'

He sat quietly while he thought. He knew he would have to do something. He was at a disadvantage, on the other side of the world, away from the publicity juggernaut that was Hollywood. He'd have to go on the attack. His father, the military general, would be pleased, he thought wryly.

'All right, I'll go along with this but I have one condition.'

Philippa nodded.

'I get to choose my fiancée…'

'Of course.' Philippa started to gather up the sheaf of actress biographies that Oliver had discarded but he shook his head.

'… But not from those.' He knew what he wanted. Whom he wanted. 'I want it to be Kat.'

'The girl downstairs?'

'Yes. It will be far more believable to think I've fallen in love with someone in Australia rather than with a Hollywood actress who I've absolutely no history with.'

'Give me some credit,' Philippa argued. 'If you have a look through those bios you'll see several women in there with whom you have been romantically linked in the past.' She shrugged. 'I'll say you rekindled an old flame.'

'No,' Oliver insisted. 'It will be better if she's not a celebrity. There's no dirt to dig up.'

'Are you sure?'

He wasn't sure at all. Not about Philippa's plan and not about getting Kat to agree—but admitting that would get him nowhere. 'Yes. Trust me. I can do this.'

'Yes, I don't doubt that. But can she?'

Would she? was actually the question. 'There's only one way to find out,' he said as he stood up. 'I'll go and get her.'

Oliver closed his eyes and rested his head on the wall of the lift as it descended to the lobby. How did he tell Kat about this? What if she believed that he was to blame for Natalie's death? What if she believed he had a history of drug use? He knew she wouldn't abide that. He knew she'd be disappointed in him and that was the last thing he wanted.

She was sitting at a table by the window, flicking through a magazine. He sat opposite her and reached for her hands, an apology ready. 'Kat, I'm sorry about that.'

'Is everything OK?'

'Not really. Can you come upstairs? I'll explain then.'

Kat followed without question and Oliver let himself breathe again. Maybe it would be OK.

He opened the door to their suite and held it for her. 'Philippa is still here,' he warned, 'and there's something I need to ask you.'

Kat looked wary. 'What's going on?' She was looking from him to Philippa and back to him again.

'Oliver needs a fake fiancée for a fake engagement—'

'Philippa! Please.' Oliver held up a hand. 'I'll handle this.'

Kat's wary expression changed to one of confusion. 'Handle what exactly?'

Oliver still had hold of her hand. He led her to the sofa in the sitting room. He sat on the edge of the coffee table, his knees touching hers. 'Apparently I'm in the headlines again. You remember we spoke about the girl who died of a drug overdose at my house?'

Kat nodded.

'Her parents are suing me. They're saying their daughter didn't have a drug problem and that as the owner of the property I am partly responsible for her death.'

'Are you?'

'No. I told you I wasn't there.'

'Where did the drugs come from?'

'I have no idea. Not from me. I have never touched illegal drugs.'

He saw her glance down at the coffee table. The photo of Natalie's smiling face was poking out from under the pile of papers, touching his thigh.

She picked up the photo. 'Is this her?'

Oliver nodded.

'Do you think they have a case against you?'

'I don't know.'

'Oliver's lawyer will have something to say,' Philippa said.

Kat looked at Oliver enquiringly.

'I have to argue this. I can't stay silent. I am innocent.'

Kat was quiet. Oliver waited anxiously, his heart lodged in his throat, to see if she was going to believe him.

'What if they win? What happens then? It doesn't bring their daughter back,' she said.

'They want money,' Philippa replied. 'If they won there would be a financial settlement, but that's not really the problem. If they win it could ruin Oliver's career.'

'What are you going to do?' Kat looked at Oliver.

'We're in damage control,' Philippa interjected. 'Oliver will refute the charges but he also needs something to boost his image, to maintain his appeal. Something to counteract any negative publicity. He needs something to make him look like a saint, not a sinner.'

'And what does this have to do with me?' Kat looked at Oliver.

'I want you to marry me.'

'Marry you?'

He hadn't just said that, had he? That wasn't what he'd meant to say. He was *sure* that wasn't what he'd meant to say.

'You don't have to actually get married,' Philippa responded. 'Just agree to be engaged.'

'And that would entail what exactly?' Kat's tone was frosty.

'Pose for some photos together. Maybe give a couple of joint interviews.'

'Why me?'

'It makes sense,' Oliver told her. 'We can have a whirlwind romance.' It wouldn't be difficult at all to pretend to be in love with Kat. She was gorgeous, kind, smart, and he liked who he was when he was around her. She made him a much better version of himself. He wanted her to think highly of him, he wanted her to respect him.

He didn't want this lawsuit to paint him in a bad light, not to his fans but especially not to Kat. She was becoming important to him. Asking her to be his fake fiancée did make sense, but that wasn't his primary motivator. He couldn't imagine asking anyone else. But he was hesitant to tell her his real reasons. He wasn't sure if he could handle hearing her thoughts. What if she thought he was a disappointment?

'That's a good idea,' Philippa finally agreed. 'You can say you fell head over heels, madly in love the moment you met. It was love at first sight. The fans will lap that up. At least the ones who didn't dream of marrying you themselves. They'll be hoping it all falls through.'

Oliver looked at Kat. She didn't look impressed. 'I don't think you're helping, Philippa,' he said before doing his best to get Kat on board. He really didn't want to pretend to be engaged to anyone but her. 'Kat, it'll be fine. When we get back to Coober Pedy we'll be tucked away in the middle of the desert, so you don't have to worry about crazy fans—I don't think even my craziest fans would find us there.'

'You actually have fans who stalk you?'

'On occasion. But I'll look after you. And this is only temporary. Please?'

'That's right,' Philippa spoke up again, 'it's only temporary. Just continue with the story until this gets sorted. I'll organise everything for your public engagements, your wardrobe, hair, make-up et cetera for any interviews and photo shoots, and you'll be financially compensated for your time and inconvenience.'

'You're going to pay me?'

'Of course. Think of your assistance as being a service for hire, if you will.'

Kat wished Philippa would stop talking. The more she spoke, the more incensed Kat became. She couldn't believe Oliver's publicist thought this was a good idea.

She turned to Oliver to give him a piece of her mind, but he looked devastated. With the exception of when he was acting, she'd only ever seen him in a good mood. Seeing him so despondent gave her pause for thought. 'Is this the best idea you could come up with?'

'Yes,' Philippa answered, even though Kat's question had been directed at Oliver.

She kept her gaze focused on him.

'I'm not sure. It would work,' he paused, 'but whether it's the only option or the best one, I don't know.'

'Why would you choose me?'

'Because I think it's the most believable scenario. I wasn't in a serious relationship when I left the States, so for me to suddenly become engaged it needs to be to someone I've met in Australia. I know you better than anyone else here. But you need to be comfortable with the idea.'

'Can I have some time to think about it?'

Oliver looked at Philippa, reminding Kat again that the whole exercise was staged. Like Oliver's life, everything was manipulated for publicity, for the media, for the fans. Her life was so simple and straightforward by comparison. Would she be able to pull this off? Did she want to?

'We have a little bit of time,' Philippa said. 'It's the middle of the night back home. Your lawyer will make a start on getting character statements about you and he'll look into Natalie's past as well. Can I leave it with you to discuss and let me know tomorrow? I've booked into this hotel too.'

Oliver nodded and showed Philippa out of the suite.

Kat remained on the couch. Stunned. She wasn't sure what to think and even less certain about what to do.

'Are you OK?'

'I'm not sure I understand what just happened.'

'I need your help.'

'That bit I understand, but I need some time to get my head around it.'

Oliver's phone pinged with a text message,

distracting them both. She was relieved; she didn't want to talk about the situation right now.

Oliver took his phone from his pocket and looked at the screen. 'It's George; he's out of Recovery and ready for visitors. Did you still want to come or would you rather stay here?'

She didn't want to stay behind. Going to the hospital would give her something to do, something else to think about. 'I'll come with you.'

'I don't want to mention this lawsuit to George. Not yet. He's got enough to worry about.'

Kat nodded. That suited her. She didn't know how they would explain the situation they were in.

She was pleased to find George in good spirits after his laparoscopic surgery to remove his gall bladder. He was alert and his pain seemed to be under control.

'What's the story, George?' Oliver asked. 'How long before we're back filming?'

'Apparently I can be discharged once my pain is under control and I can move about comfortably. I think I should be back on deck at the end of the week.'

'Did you tell the doctor you'll be going back to Coober Pedy?' Kat asked.

'I said "on location". And that I need to fly. The airline will need a letter from her giving me permission to fly and I need to have someone accompany me.'

'We can do that, can't we, Kat?' Oliver asked. 'We've got to fly back at some point.'

Kat wasn't sure they should rush it. She turned to George. 'It's one thing being comfortable in hospital in the city, George, but it's another thing being in the desert, five hundred kilometres from town.'

'Days off are costing the studio money,' he replied. 'I promise I'll follow medical advice. I'll sit in a chair and direct. You can keep an eye on me.'

'I can't be there twenty-four-seven,' Kat said as she refilled George's glass from the water jug on his bedside table.

George gestured at the jug as Kat emptied it. 'Oliver, could you please find a nurse and see if I can have my water jug refilled?' He waited until Oliver had left the room before turning back to Kat. 'What did he mean, "We've got to fly back at some point"? What's this "we" business? Why are you here? I meant it when I told you to stay away from him, Kat. I don't want you getting hurt.'

'It's OK, George. I can handle it. I'm not going to get my heart broken.'

Thank God they hadn't mentioned the latest development and Oliver's proposal. She hated to think what George would have to say about that. Agreeing to Oliver's request would be the antithesis of staying away from him. A holiday fling was one thing; pretending to be his fiancée was another. The more she thought about it, the more she thought she couldn't do it. She'd have to tell Oliver.

'Oliver and I have decided we've had enough drama,' she continued as Oliver came back into the room; she didn't want him to think they'd been discussing him behind his back, 'so if you promise you will take it easy and can stay out of hospital, I'll agree to be responsible for your health.'

'I know you think I have a chequered medical history but I am normally, fit and healthy.'

'So it's just when I'm around, then?'

'Seems to be.'

'You never did tell me how you two met,' Oliver said as he looked from one of them to the other.

'I was scouting some bush locations in the Adelaide Hills years ago. I twisted my knee and tore some ligaments and had to be carried out. Poor Kat was one of the paramedics at the scene. We got talking about where I'd filmed, what I was looking for. Kat told me about several films that had been shot in Coober Pedy. I'd heard of it, of course, but had never been. I was keen to film there, so when this movie got off the ground I got in touch with Kat to see what connections she had.'

'I told him I'd moved back to town.'

'And the rest is history.'

Their third day in Adelaide began just as perfectly as the others. Oliver hadn't pressed her for her answer yet. He'd planned a day's outing for them and was keen to get on the road. Kat didn't argue. She didn't want to tell him her decision, not yet; she didn't want to disappoint him and potentially taint their last day in the city.

Oliver had organised a car and a driver through the hotel and Kat was enjoying being chauffeured around the Fleurieu Peninsula. Oliver had wanted to get out into the country and see something green, so they had visited a couple of wineries in McLaren Vale, played tourist at the weird and wonderful d'Arenberg Cube, before stopping for lunch at a clifftop restaurant recommended by the hotel concierge that overlooked the beach at Port Willunga.

They were seated on the veranda of the restaurant looking over the water. Oliver had his sunglasses on, hiding his distinctive blue eyes. Kat knew he wanted the anonymity today and the sun was high in the sky, reflecting brightly off the water, making sunglasses kind of mandatory, but she wished he'd take them off. She loved being able to look into his eyes.

Kat couldn't believe people actually lived like this—chauffeured cars, five-star hotels, sipping champagne on an ocean-side cliff-top. Oliver's future, legitimate fiancée would be a lucky woman.

She knew she couldn't avoid the topic any longer. He had been patient but she suspected Philippa would be less so. She knew she'd be expecting an answer the moment they arrived back at the hotel.

She'd spent many hours last night imagining what it would be like to be engaged to him. It was all too easy to imagine and that was when she knew she really couldn't agree to his proposal.

'We need to talk about your request,' she said.

'Have you made a decision?'

She nodded. 'I don't think I can do it.'

'Why not?'

She knew her feelings for him were all too

real and she was terrified he'd see that. She couldn't act, and if she played her part convincingly he might figure out that she had fallen for him. She couldn't allow that to happen. They were too different. They had no future and it was best if she didn't get any more involved. She was starting to worry that she wouldn't get out with her heart intact, and playing the part of his fiancée would only make things harder. But she needed a reason that she could give him. 'What if I'm not convincing enough? If people see through me that won't help your case. It'll make us both look ridiculous. If I don't do it, will you be able to find someone else?'

'Yes. Philippa had some ideas. She'll pick someone. I told you it was totally your decision.'

She'd half hoped he'd try to talk her round. But she knew he'd only do that if this was real, not make-believe. She knew she was replaceable. She knew Philippa had several other possible candidates to put in front of Oliver. He'd said he wanted her, but that didn't mean he needed her. He just needed someone. He was smart enough to know there was no point in coercing a fake fiancée into playing the role. That would never work.

He accepted her decision without argument

and Kat tried to hide her disappointment. It had been her choice after all.

The waitress had cleared their plates that now showed no traces of the freshly caught King George whiting they'd devoured. Oliver ordered coffee as Kat's mobile vibrated on the table. She glanced at it without intending to pick it up. It was Saskia. She'd call her back.

The phone stopped ringing but buzzed almost immediately with a text message.

Call me—urgent.

Her heart plummeted as icy fingers gripped it and tugged it lower in her chest. Waves of cold fear ran through her. Saskia knew where she was, she'd encouraged her to go with Oliver, and Kat knew she wouldn't interrupt without good reason.

'It's Saskia,' she said as she picked up her phone and showed Oliver the text message. 'I have to call her.'

Oliver nodded.

Kat took her phone outside. She was aware that Oliver stood as she did but he didn't follow her.

She pressed redial and stood on the cliffs at Port Willunga, facing the ocean but not seeing it as she waited for the call to connect and

Saskia to answer. It was a glorious day but Kat couldn't focus on anything, her thoughts scrambling in her head as she tried to guess what was wrong. She was desperate for her call to be answered.

'Sas? What is it? Is it Papa?' she said the moment the call connected.

'He's OK.' Saskia immediately tried to quell Kat's rising panic. 'He's on his way to Port Augusta with the flying doctor.'

'What happened?'

'He had a heart attack.'

'What? When?'

'This morning.'

Oh, God. Why had she agreed to come away with Oliver? What was she doing in Adelaide? Her father needed her.

'How is he?' What if he didn't make it? What if she lost him too? Her family was everything to her.

'He's stable. But we'll know more when he gets to Port Augusta. I thought you might want to meet him there.'

'Of course I do. I'll go to the airport now. Has someone gone with him?'

'Rosa has.'

'Can you message Zia Rosa, tell her I'm on my way?'

'OK. Call me later. I love you.'

'Love you too…thanks, Sas.'

'On your way where? What's happened?' Oliver was beside her. She hadn't noticed him come out of the restaurant.

'It's my dad. He's had a heart attack.' Her voice caught on a sob. 'He's being flown to Port Augusta. I need to get there.'

The driver pulled up beside them as Kat finished speaking. Oliver held the car door open for her. 'Hop in. I've paid the bill—we can go straight to the airport.'

She didn't ask how he knew what needed to be done; she was incapable of thinking logically. She was just grateful that he was there and was willing and able to sort things out. Someone needed to take control and her muddled brain wasn't capable of thinking of anything but getting to Port Augusta. The actual logistics of the trip were beyond her.

'Can you look up flights to Port Augusta for me? I have no idea when the next one will be.'

'I'll call the hotel. They can organise it for us.'

Oliver had his mobile phone in his hand. 'It's Frank Foster,' he said.

Kat was only half listening. She heard something about a plane and bags.

She kept her eyes locked onto her phone,

waiting in vain for an update from someone.
Anyone.

'How long does it take the flying doctor to
reach Port Augusta?' Oliver asked her.

'An hour.'

'So, they're unlikely to be there yet,' he said
gently, taking her phone and turning it face
down in her lap. 'I'm sure your aunt will call
you as soon as she can.'

'What if I don't get there in time?'

'I'll make sure you do. I have a plan. I'm
sure everything will be all right.'

'But what if it's not?' Her voice wobbled. 'I
was in Adelaide when my mum passed away.
I can't go through that again.'

'Kat.' Oliver turned in his seat to face her.
He picked up her hands and his touch calmed
her, reassured her. 'Saskia said he was stable.
He's in the hands of the flying doctors on his
way to specialist care. You have to trust them
to do their job and trust me to get you there.
Do you?' He continued when she nodded.
'And is there anything else you could have
done for him if you'd been there? Other than
what is happening now?'

'No.' She shook her head.

'So, take a breath. I'll get you there as soon
as I can.'

She took his advice and tried her best to

relax. She was glad Oliver was with her. When she'd been in this position last time, when she'd received the phone call with the news that her mum had been in a car accident, she'd been alone. This was better.

The car called past the hotel where the concierge was waiting with Kat's bags, as Oliver had arranged, before continuing on to the airport. Kat grew more edgy as they approached the airport. She hoped there wouldn't be any delays with the flight to Port Augusta, no late passengers, no mechanical or security issues. Every minute counted.

The driver pulled to a stop well before the main terminal. Oliver had the door open almost before the wheels had finished turning.

'Why are we getting out here?' Kat asked. The entrance to the terminal was still several hundred metres ahead of them.

'I've booked us a private plane. We can go straight onto the apron. It's waiting for us. It'll take off as soon as we get there.'

'A private plane?'

'It's the fastest way of getting us there. Call your aunt—let her know you're on the way.'

Oliver took Kat's luggage from the driver as she nodded and brought her aunt's number up on the phone. She walked as she talked, disconnecting as Oliver introduced himself to the pilot and they walked out onto the tarmac.

'How is he?' Oliver asked as the pilot stowed Kat's luggage.

'Stable. My aunt will text any updates while I'm in the air.'

'Good news. Let's get going.'

'You're coming with me?' Kat asked as Oliver stepped onto the stairs behind her.

He nodded. 'I didn't think you were in any state to be sent off alone. You don't mind, do you? I didn't think you'd want to be alone with all your thoughts. I won't interfere at the hospital, I'll just see you safely there.'

Of course he wouldn't interfere at the hospital—he didn't do family.

'No, I don't mind. I'd love some company.'

'Good. I'll come back to Adelaide later, once I know you're OK, so that I'm back to accompany George when he's discharged, as promised.'

'I don't know how to thank you,' she said as she collapsed into the seat and felt the plane immediately begin to taxi.

Oliver handed her a bottle of water from the fridge. 'You don't need to thank me. I'm pleased I could do this for you.'

The leather seats were large and comfortable, the air-conditioning was just the right temperature and the bottled water refreshing. Oliver sat beside her and wrapped his arm around her shoulder, holding her close. Kat closed her eyes and finally let herself relax. She was on the way. Oliver had got her this far; there was nothing more she could do right now.

Kat hesitated at the entrance to the hospital emergency department. She could see her aunt Rosa in the waiting area. She didn't want to introduce her to Oliver. Not now. She didn't want to explain who he was and why she was with him. She didn't want distractions.

She turned to Oliver. 'Thank you for all your help. That's my aunt Rosa over there. I can manage from here.'

'You'll be OK?'

Oliver couldn't hide the look of disappointment on his face. She felt terrible for brushing him off but she couldn't deal with any introductions at the moment. He'd told her he didn't do family. He couldn't expect to meet any more of hers. Not now. Not today.

She nodded. She couldn't worry if she'd upset him. She didn't have room in her head to worry about his feelings.

Oliver's breath was coming in short, sharp bursts, keeping time with his fists as he punched into the boxing pads Chris held in front of him. Thwack, thwack, grunt, breathe.

'Take it easy, buddy, you've got to look after that strained rib muscle.'

Oliver could feel the muscle complain every time he landed a punch, but he welcomed the pain. It kept him focused on the exercise, it kept his mind off Kat. A solid session in the gym was the only way to exhaust him. It meant he could collapse into bed at the end of the day and hopefully get some sleep.

'I reckon that will do for today,' Chris said, allowing Oliver one more punch. 'You can cool down on the bike.'

Oliver wasn't ready to call it quits. Not on the session and not on Kat. He picked up his towel and wiped the sweat from his face and neck. He'd go for a run on the treadmill and then cool off.

He cranked the treadmill up, jogging at a pace to keep his heart rate elevated, but the exercise didn't require his full concentration and his mind, inevitably, turned to Kat. He hadn't seen her for three days. She was still in Port Augusta, with her father, who was recovering after heart surgery. She hadn't told Oliver when she'd be back. He hadn't asked.

They'd communicated via text message. He hadn't known what was expected of him.

She'd refused to be his fake fiancée but he wasn't really sure why. He could only assume she didn't want to be associated with him and any rumours. He could only assume she was disappointed in him and the situations he found himself in.

She said she believed him, but what if she didn't? Her opinion was important to him. *She* was important to him but he didn't know what to do about that. She had shut him out and he knew he couldn't go after her. He had to move on. With a fake fiancée.

He'd offered to help get Kat to Port Augusta because he could and because he wanted to. He wanted to help her and he also wanted to prove to her that he was capable of thinking about someone other than himself. Something other than his career. But he knew his offer hadn't been completely altruistic. He had hoped it might help her to see past some of his mistakes. Had hoped it might help her to change her mind about him.

But it hadn't helped. She'd sent him away. She hadn't wanted to introduce him to her aunt or her father. He understood it was a stressful time for her but he'd mistakenly, stupidly, thought that he could help ease that stress. That his presence would provide some comfort.

He'd told her he understood her decision not to be his fake fiancée, but it had stung.

She had rejected him.

And now he had to choose someone else to 'propose' to but it was a decision he'd been delaying. Not only because he didn't want it to be someone else but also because it would mean the end of his time with Kat. Once he had a fiancée in the eyes of the world his time spent with Kat would be over. It would have to be.

Philippa had been hounding him to make a decision and he'd promised her an answer tomorrow, but he still couldn't see past Kat. If he needed a fiancée, he still wanted it to be her. It didn't matter how many times he told himself that he'd manage, that he could live without her, he couldn't get her out of his head.

He missed her.

He decreased the speed on the treadmill, slowing it to a walk. He'd go back to his room, shower and have another look at those photos from Philippa. He'd choose someone else and try to forget about Kat. He obviously had stronger feelings for her than she did for him.

He'd made a mistake.

He'd focus on the movie. On his career. Just as he'd always done. Only he knew he'd lost some of the enjoyment that he usually got from work. It was no longer enough to keep him satisfied. He needed Kat.

Kat looked out of the window of the plane at the ochre earth and pale mullock heaps that dotted the landscape. She was relieved to be coming home and relieved that her father was recovering well following surgery to insert a stent into his blocked artery. She had a lot to be grateful for.

Normally she'd be pleased to see the familiar landscape but she had other things on her mind today. She was eager for the plane to land, eager to be home, but more eager to see Oliver. She'd missed his company over the past few days and she intended to head straight to the film set once she'd picked up her car. She needed an Oliver fix and she had something to tell him.

He'd texted her asking after her dad but hadn't intruded. She hadn't asked if he was keeping his distance deliberately or whether a text message was the level of communication he was happy with when it came to discussing her family. She'd been pleased to hear from him but appreciated that he hadn't pushed her. She'd wanted to be able to concentrate on her father without distractions. But now she was keen to see him. Her father was being trans-

ferred by ambulance home to Coober Pedy
and was going to make a full recovery; she
didn't need to feel guilty about spending time
with Oliver.

She thanked God for Oliver and his calm, un-
flappable personality when she'd needed to get
to her father's side quickly. For someone who
knew how to have a good time it was reassur-
ing to see that it wasn't all about red carpets,
private jets and five-star luxury. She'd known
he had a good work ethic, she'd seen plenty
of evidence of that, but to see such a compassionate side was something special. And it had
made her rethink what he'd asked of her.

He had been there for her when she needed
him. It was her turn to do the same for him.

She was excited to see him. She'd missed
how he made her feel—beautiful, special and
fun. He'd shown her there was more to life
than working and living here. She didn't want
to be disappointed by her life but she wondered how she would go back to normal once
he'd left. There'd be no more five-star hotels,
no more karaoke serenades, private jets or
amazing sex. She suspected he would move
on without a backward glance but she doubted
she'd be able to do the same. She imagined

things would never be quite the same for her again.

She drove out to the film set, the cluster of dusty trailers, marquees and huts in the desert a familiar sight to her now. She parked and headed straight to his trailer. If he wasn't there she'd search elsewhere.

She knocked on his door and was relieved when it opened, and her heart leapt in her chest when she saw him standing there. She'd almost forgotten how gorgeous he was.

'Kat! You're back!' He stepped towards her and she expected him to greet her with a kiss but he stopped in his tracks, stepped back and held the door open wider. 'Come in.'

She stepped inside and saw Philippa sitting on the couch. Was that why he'd held himself back?

'We're just in the middle of something.'

'Actually, I needed to see both of you.' She'd wanted to see Oliver first but her news did involve them both. She might as well tell them together.

Philippa was shuffling through some papers on the coffee table, her movements drawing Kat's eye. She could see pages of photos spread out on the table. Had he picked another fake fiancée? Of course he had.

'Have you chosen someone else?' she asked.

She hadn't imagined this scenario. Why hadn't she? She should have known. She'd been stupid. He wouldn't need her now.

'Yes,' said Philippa.

'Why?' asked Oliver.

Oliver hadn't said yes. Maybe there was still a chance he needed her. 'I came to tell you I would do it.'

'Really?' Oliver was staring at her.

'If you still need me.'

'Yes! Definitely.' His smile stretched across his mouth, from one corner to the other, and Kat knew she'd made the right decision.

'I do have one condition,' she added. She waited for both Oliver and Philippa to nod, to show they were at least paying attention. 'I want you to donate any money that you were happy to pay me to the Coober Pedy drive-in, to go towards the upgrading of the facilities. It can be a donation on behalf of Oliver to the town.' She didn't want any remuneration but she had decided this was one thing she could do, one way she could make sure something else positive came out of this. It would be a win for the town and she could sell it as being a grand gesture on Oliver's part. Maybe it would get him some more positive publicity.

'Done.' Philippa didn't hesitate and Kat wondered if she should have named a price.

'And I want another donation to the flying doctor service too,' she said, hoping she hadn't overstepped the mark.

'No problem,' Philippa replied.

'Are you sure you're OK with this?' Oliver asked her. There was the smallest of creases between his blue eyes. He looked worried. She didn't think she'd seen him look worried before. He was normally so full of confidence, so carefree.

She wasn't sure she could pull it off but she knew she wanted to try. She wanted to help. 'Do you really think we can convince people to believe we're in love?'

'Oliver is an actor,' said Philippa. 'It's his job to make people believe.'

'But I'm *not* an actor—do you think I'll be able to do this?'

'I don't; you were Oliver's choice. If you think it's too much for you to handle then I have plenty of other potential fiancées for him.'

Kat was not about to let Philippa get the better of her. She remembered Oliver's words— he wasn't one to back down from a challenge. Neither was she. It wouldn't be hard to pretend to be in love with Oliver. Not too hard at all.

'I want it to be you, Kat.' Oliver reached for her and her body came alive at his touch.

'We can do this.' His blue gaze locked her in place. Their hips were touching. He ran his hands down her upper arms and Kat breathed in deeply as her insides trembled. 'I don't want to do this without you. Are we good?'

She nodded, incapable of speech while his eyes held her attention and his hands held her elbows.

He bent his head and Kat closed her eyes as his lips touched hers. Softly, lightly, a gentle caress.

'Thank you,' he said as he lifted his head, leaving Kat to wonder which kiss that was. It didn't matter, it had been just what she'd wanted. Exactly what she needed.

'I'll take you to dinner tonight,' he said, 'just the two of us—we need some time to sort out how this is going to work—but now I have to get back on set. Can you meet me at the hotel at seven-thirty? I'll book a table in Mona's restaurant.'

She nodded. She could do this and she'd worry about the consequences later.

Kat dressed carefully, it wasn't every day she got engaged. Even if it was all a charade having dinner at Mona's was reason enough to dress up.

She stepped into the red trouser suit she'd

bought in Adelaide. That Oliver had bought
her. He'd seen it in a shop window on Jetty
Road and had insisted she try it on. He'd said
the colour red would always remind him of
her. She'd protested that she had nowhere to
wear it, it was far too smart for anywhere she
went in Coober Pedy, *and* it was too expensive. Oliver had told her she looked beautiful
and had bought it for her.

She zipped it up and looked in the mirror.
She had to admit it fitted her well but if she
hadn't been meeting Oliver she doubted she
would have had the confidence to wear head-
to-toe red. It was such a bold statement. But
Oliver gave her confidence. She recalled the
admiration in his eyes when he'd first seen her
in this outfit and she crossed her fingers that
he'd like it just as much tonight.

He was waiting for her in the hotel lobby. He
smiled and took her hands, holding them wide
apart as he looked at her. His eyes were bright
as he said, 'You look sensational.'

He did too. He had also dressed up and wore
pale cotton trousers, a pale blue dress shirt and
a navy jacket. He had no tie and wore leather
shoes, without socks. He looked as if he'd
walked off the page of a fashion catalogue.

He stepped in close and let go of her hands. He put his fingers under her chin, tipping her face up to him and kissing her on the lips. Kat felt the now familiar flutters in her belly as the touch of his lips warmed her from the inside.

'Are you hungry?'

She nodded. He took her hand and she walked beside him towards the restaurant. It was only past the bar, further into the hotel, further underground, but it took them several minutes as several hotel guests requested selfies with Oliver. He asked Kat if she minded, which she didn't, before he posed happily with fans.

When they eventually made it into the restaurant he asked for the quietest table, away from curious ears but still within sight of other diners. He was acting as though he didn't have a care in the world.

'Aren't you worried about the lawsuit?' Kat asked after the waiter had taken their order.

Oliver shook his head. 'I feel sick when I think about what happened to Natalie; she shouldn't have died and I feel terrible that it happened in my house, but it wasn't my fault and I have confidence in my legal team. I admit I've had my fair share of headlines over the years and this is right up there in the scale of monumental disasters, but I know I did nothing wrong. I believe justice will be done. I can't imagine what it must be like for Natalie's parents and I feel for them, I really do, but I'm not going to be made the scapegoat.

'I am not going to let them ruin my reputation or my career. It's one thing to have a reputation as a playboy, another one entirely to be implicated in an accidental death.'

'I know I agreed to be your fake fiancée until you're off the hook,' she said as the waiter brought their meal and Oliver ordered more drinks, 'but do you have any idea how long that might take?' Kat didn't know how successful she'd be in pulling off the role of a fake fiancée, or, more to the point, she was worried that the longer their plan lasted, the more difficulty she'd have separating fact from fiction.

'I'm hoping not long. I want to get it settled and out of the papers. I've spoken to my lawyer. He's got several statements and photographs of Natalie which seem to contradict her parents' claim that she never touched drugs. I feel bad that he has investigators trawling through her private life but her parents instigated this and my lawyer thinks he will have enough evidence soon to get Natalie's parents to drop the lawsuit. I can't thank you enough for what you're doing for me but it shouldn't be for too long. Is that OK?'

She nodded.

'Thank you. I owe you a favour. Two probably.'

'I'll let you pay for dinner.' She smiled, relieved to hear him being so positive about the situation.

'I was going to, and that only takes care of one favour.'

'I'll think of something else,' she said, knowing exactly what she would ask for.

'Good,' Oliver said just as the waiter appeared with a bottle of champagne. 'I want to propose a toast.'

'What are we toasting?' Kat asked as Oliver handed her the glass that had been poured.

'To a successful partnership.' He smiled and touched his glass to hers. 'I think we could make a good team,' he said as she sipped her champagne. 'Which brings me to another question for you.'

Before she could ask what it was Oliver had stood up from the table and dropped to one knee.

'What are you doing?' Kat almost choked on her champagne.

'Legitimising our agreement.'

Kat was aware of a lull in conversation as the other restaurant patrons all turned to watch them.

'From the moment I first saw you I was captivated but you have shown me so much more than your beauty. Not only are you beautiful, sexy and smart but you are also kind, generous, caring and loving and I need you in my life. I can only hope that you need me too and that I have some of the qualities you value in a partner. Kat, will you do me the honour of accepting my proposal of marriage?'

Kat's heart was racing and her hands were shaking but she still noticed that there was no declaration of love. There wasn't anything that could be construed any differently on her part than what it was—a fake proposal.

She knew the other patrons watching wouldn't notice. They'd only see Oliver, down on one knee, proposing. They wouldn't be listening to the words. They'd be caught up in the theatrics. After all, he was an actor. But no matter what they heard and how well Oliver played his role, she knew the engagement was fake and she needed to remember that was all it was. And she had a part to play.

CHAPTER EIGHT

OLIVER WAS STILL down on one knee, waiting. The restaurant was silent, the other patrons all waiting too.

Kat wasn't used to such a public display and the attention made her mind go blank. She had no idea what her lines were. She wasn't used to this at all. She felt tears in her eyes but, while they lent authenticity to the spectacle, she had no idea why she was crying.

Somehow, she managed to nod and suddenly applause rippled around them as Oliver sprang up from his knees and gathered her into his arms and kissed her. Despite her knowing his proposal was a sham, his kisses felt real and Kat took some comfort from that. Being kissed by Oliver was a memory no one could take away from her. That was something she could keep.

She was aware of a barrage of camera flashes as people recorded and photographed

Oliver's proposal. She knew the pictures would be uploaded to social media, and perhaps it was all part of the plan—if not Oliver's then definitely Philippa's. She understood this was what she'd signed up for: Oliver needed the positive publicity.

The applause died down when they sat. Oliver topped up their champagne glasses before reaching behind him, into the pocket of his jacket. When he turned back to Kat he held a small velvet box in the palm of his hand. He flipped open the lid.

Nestled inside was a diamond ring. Teardrop-shaped, in a high claw setting, it was enormous, stunning but totally impractical in the rough and tumble outback and seemed even more so to Kat when she considered her job. She needed something that was tough, that could withstand getting knocked and wouldn't tear into the rubber gloves she was always pulling on for work. She would have chosen a bezel setting and would have preferred an opal.

'Where did this come from?'

'Philippa picked it out this afternoon.'

His proposal might have felt real but it didn't take much to shatter the illusion. Six little words.

Someone else had chosen the ring.

He picked up her left hand and slid the ring onto her fourth finger. It was a perfect fit. The deal was done.

A final burst of camera flashes lit up the room.

Kat looked around nervously. 'The news will be well and truly out before I make it home tonight—you'd better hope my father doesn't hear about this before I have a chance to explain.' She needed to tell her family what was going on. She realised, too late, she should have warned them already.

'I would like to be there when you tell him.'

'Why?'

'Because it's the right thing to do. It's courteous and one thing I've never been accused of is having poor manners. And it's important that I meet your father if we're going to manage to sell this story to the media.'

He was right. Her whole family needed to meet him and she could use his support when she told them of the arrangement. She wasn't sure how they would react to this news. 'You could come to dinner tomorrow.'

'Your weekly family dinner?' He sounded worried.

'It's at Dean and Saskia's...but if you don't think you can handle it...'

'I'll be fine.'

* * *

Saskia greeted them at the door and Oliver relaxed slightly. Saskia was a familiar face at least.

He didn't do family but he knew he had to make an exception in this case. Even though he and Kat were only posing as a newly engaged couple, he knew it was important that he meet Kat's father and make sure he got him on side.

But the warm greeting he'd hoped for wasn't forthcoming. Saskia barely acknowledged either of them and if she said 'hello' he must have missed it. She pulled Kat inside and whispered, rather loudly, 'I can't believe you didn't tell us, Kat. It's all over the internet.'

Saskia was brandishing her mobile phone and, without pausing, tapped it and held it up so they could see the screen. A video of Oliver's proposal, recorded by a restaurant patron last night and uploaded to the internet, was running.

Kat's face went pale. 'Does Papa know? Has he seen this?'

Saskia shook her head. 'No.'

'It's not what you think.'

'What does that mean?'

'I'll tell you after we've spoken to Papa.'

Saskia picked up Kat's left hand. 'Where's the ring?'

Her hand was bare.

'In my purse. I was worried about damaging it.'

Oliver knew she was thinking the ring had to be returned. He was finding he was attuned to her thoughts and often knew what she was going to say before she spoke. He was an experienced observer of people, their mannerisms, gaits and habits—it all helped when he was trying to build a character. He was a good mimic of accents too but, while he listened to *how* people spoke, he didn't always listen to what they said. It was different with Kat. *He* was different with Kat.

Kat was definitely upset, obviously worried about her father's reaction to their news, and Oliver's own nerves intensified. He hoped he could pull this off. And he hoped it wasn't a mistake to be meeting Kat's family en masse. To be breaking this news to them collectively.

He was tense as Saskia led them into the house and Kat introduced him to her father. Tony did not look impressed. Kat had warned him on several occasions about her protective father. Oliver just hoped he gave him a chance.

'Papa, this is Oliver Harding. Oliver, this is my father, Tony.'

Oliver extended his hand. 'It's a pleasure to meet you, sir.'

Tony's handshake was firm, his palm rough. He looked Oliver up and down, taking in his neatly pressed clothes, his soft leather shoes, his manicured nails. Oliver was certain he didn't approve and it bothered him. He wanted Kat's father to like him. He knew Kat would be influenced by her family's perceptions of him and he didn't want anything they said or thought to make Kat think less of him.

'You're an actor.'

It was a statement, delivered as though Tony felt actors were on a par with axe murderers.

'Yes, I am.' He wasn't going to apologise for his career choice. He was good at his craft and he made a very good living. He was successful.

'And American.'

'Papa!'

'Settle down, Katarina; an American is as welcome for dinner as the next person. What would you like to drink, Oliver? Will you have a beer?'

'That sounds good, thank you.'

Maybe the night would go better than expected, Oliver thought as he accepted a drink and was introduced to Roger's wife, Maya, as well as Kat's aunt Rosa. Despite doing his best over the years to avoid families—both his own and anyone else's—he found it was nice to be able to put faces to the names that he'd heard so often from Kat.

The family gathered in the spacious living room; although Kat had described their underground houses to him, he was still surprised by the size of the rooms and the height of the ceilings. The room was large and airy with one window that looked out into the front 'garden', which was really just more bare earth with a couple of native eucalyptus trees, an outdoor seating area and a barbecue. Along with the adults, there were several children who ran in and out of the room, interested only in the food that was laid out on the coffee table, but even when Saskia sent them off with their own bowls of crisps the conversational noise level was still high.

Until Kat said, 'Papa, we have some news.'

The noise level in the room dropped immediately, almost as if someone had flipped a switch or pulled a plug. Five pairs of eyes swivelled in their direction. Even though Kat had spoken, Oliver was aware that a lot of the attention was focused on him. Kat had said 'we' and it was obvious her family were keen to hear what was coming next, and Oliver knew they would be gunning for him if they didn't like what they heard.

'It's nothing to get excited about but we wanted to tell you before you heard anything on the grapevine. Oliver and I are engaged.'

'What?' Tony was looking from Kat to Oliver as if he couldn't believe what he was hearing. Oliver and Kat were sitting on the same couch, not touching, and there was a good several inches between them, but even so, Oliver got the impression that Kat's father would very much like to pick him up and put him on another chair, far away from Kat, in another room even.

Oliver was watching Tony but out of the corner of his eye he could see both Roger and Dean. He noticed that they both sat up a little straighter in their chairs, waiting for Tony's reaction, waiting to see if they needed to spring into action. Pick Oliver up and throw him out of the house, perhaps? Oliver didn't doubt that between the two of them they'd have no trouble managing that.

'You're going to marry a man I've never met, and you,' he turned to Oliver, staring him down, 'you didn't have the decency to come to see me first.'

Oliver wondered if he was joking. His expression suggested he wasn't. Did he really expect that a man would still ask his potential father-in-law for permission to marry his daughter? Did people still do that? Oliver prided himself on his manners but, he had to admit, he had no idea about proper proposal etiquette.

'Papa, calm down. We're not actually going to get married.'

'What on earth does that mean? People don't get engaged to *not* get married.'

'I'm doing this as a favour for Oliver. It's for publicity. It will help his career.'

Dean and Roger were still bristling but at least they'd stayed in their seats. Saskia had excused herself earlier and was busy in the kitchen, and the only person who seemed to be on their side, judging from the sympathetic looks she was sending Kat's way, was Maya. He wasn't sure about Aunt Rosa.

'Would you like to explain exactly *how* an engagement can help a career?' Tony was addressing Kat, completely ignoring Oliver.

'Oliver needs some positive publicity. The media have got hold of a story, a false accusation, and Oliver needs something to deflect attention, something to put a positive spin on things. His publicist thinks an engagement will do the trick. I've agreed to help, just until everything settles down again.'

'And what about you? What do you get out of this arrangement?'

'You know how the Cooper Pedy Residents' Association has been fundraising for improvements for the drive-in? Oliver is going to donate money towards the upgrades and also to the flying doctors. I'm doing this for the town.'

'That's all well and good but what about your reputation? You'll have two broken engagements, Katarina. No man will marry you after that!'

Two? What was he talking about? Oliver's head was spinning as he tried to follow the rapid-fire conversation—perhaps he'd misheard. But before he had a chance to clarify just what had been said Kat was responding to her father.

'Papa, don't be ridiculous. No one even needs to know about this one.'

'Everyone *will* know about this one though, won't they?' Aunt Rosa commented. 'Isn't that the point?' Perhaps she wasn't on their side.

'Kat,' Saskia interrupted as she re-entered the room, 'have you got any balsamic vinegar at your place? I seem to have run out.'

'I'll go and have a look.'

'We'll talk about this when you get back,' Tony muttered as Kat stood up.

'Oliver, why don't you give Kat a hand?' Saskia instructed with a nod.

Oliver didn't hesitate. Saskia had given him an excuse to escape the heat and maybe both he and Tony needed a chance to rein in their tempers and digest information. Tony that his daughter was engaged, and Oliver the news that Kat was engaged *again*. He couldn't believe Kat hadn't said anything.

He followed Kat next door, the heat of the afternoon assaulting him as he left the coolness of the underground dwelling to step outside.

'You've been engaged before?' he asked as the front door closed behind him. He'd wanted a chance to see Kat's home, to be able to picture her there whenever he wanted to, but he was far too bewildered to take in his surroundings. There were other things occupying his thoughts.

'Yes.'

Oliver was astounded. He'd asked about an ex-husband, so she could have mentioned an ex-fiancé…she'd had plenty of time.

But then again, why would she have? They didn't have to know everything about each other. Even if he wanted to.

'When?'

'Six years ago. When I was in Adelaide.'

Six years! She would have been so young. 'What happened?'

He wanted to know everything, even though he was aware it wasn't really any of his business. It shouldn't matter but he was surprised to find he felt jealous. He'd wanted to be the first one to propose to her.

He knew he was being ridiculous. His proposal wasn't real, but part of him liked pretending it was.

'Mum died.' Kat's voice wobbled and Oliver felt terrible for hounding her. She'd told him about losing her mother a few years earlier. He should have remembered that and put two and two together. 'And I left Adelaide and came back here.'

'And he didn't?'

Kat shook her head and Oliver could see tears gathering on her lashes. Was she crying for her mum or for someone else?

He moved towards her, wanting to take her in his arms and comfort her, but she held up a hand. 'I'm OK,' she said and her words felt like a slap in the face. 'Adam came back with me initially but our plan was never to stay permanently. He was a vet. Is a vet. But there's no work here. Dad had his first heart scare when Mum died. Shortness of breath, difficulty breathing. We thought it was a panic attack but it was cardiac complications, so I didn't feel that I could leave him to cope with losing Mum alone. Even though he's got family living next door I didn't think it was the right thing to do and, to be honest, I didn't want to leave him. I didn't want to leave at all. I needed to have my family around me too. Adam stayed for a while but he didn't like it here. He was bored. He went back to Adelaide. I stayed.'

'For the past five years?'

'Yes.' Kat turned her back and walked into the kitchen. Oliver followed. 'In the beginning there was a lot going on. I was upset with him for leaving. I felt he didn't support me. I was struggling after Mum died and that was our first hurdle, and I figured if we couldn't get through that together there wasn't much hope for our future. Life isn't smooth sailing. I needed to know I could depend on him.

'When I needed him he wasn't there for me. He expected to be the most important person in my life, which he was, mostly, but my family needed me more, and I needed them. Adam wasn't the man I thought he was. Family comes first and there was no room in his life for my family.'

'Kat, I'm sorry, I had no idea.'

'Of course you didn't.'

'Are you sure about doing the whole engagement thing again?' Was she really prepared to have another broken engagement just to help him out, because they couldn't possibly make this work, could they? They came from two completely different worlds and he didn't intend to get married, ever. She was looking for her soulmate.

'It's fine.'

He wished she sounded more convincing but she was no actress. He could imagine how upset she would have been. He knew she wanted to find 'the one' and live happily ever after.

'Are you sure?' He really needed her to stick with the plan and, despite worrying that he might be adversely affecting her life, he really hoped she meant it. 'The whole western world will know about this, Kat. That's the point.'

'Well, it won't cause much of a ripple in Coober Pedy. You said yourself that the tabloids will move on eventually. They'll find another story. A bigger one. They won't be concerned about you, or us, for ever. It will be fine. *I'll* be fine.'

'And your father?'

'Don't worry about my father. I can handle him.'

'You shouldn't have to handle him.' He felt

responsible and therefore obligated to help. Kat shouldn't have to handle her father. 'This is my fault. I've put you in an awkward position, and I need to fix it.' He was determined to win Tony over.

'He doesn't know you. I think it's just the shock. I probably should have told him in private; maybe I could have explained things better.'

'I don't want you to bear the brunt of this. That's not fair.'

'It'll be OK; my father can be a little protective of me but I'll get him on side. We should get back,' she said, holding up the bottle of vinegar, 'before they send out a search party.'

Kat's cousins and her father were in the front, and only, garden, standing around the barbecue. Oliver knew this was his opportunity to attempt to fix things.

He knew how important family was to Kat and, if he didn't, she'd just made it perfectly clear once again. Her family came first. Their opinion mattered to her. It mattered to him too but for different reasons. He wanted to make things easier for Kat but he also needed her family to support, at least publicly, this fake engagement.

Her father and cousins were polite, offering

him another drink and making space for him at the grill, but it was clear it was going to have to be up to him to extend an olive branch. That wasn't a problem; he could do that.

'I can understand you have reservations,' he said, extending that branch, 'but I guarantee Kat won't be disadvantaged by helping me.' He wasn't expecting the barrage of questions that came flooding back to him.

'How can you be sure? You can't know her well.'

'You were obviously surprised to hear she'd been engaged before.'

'How do you expect to pull this off if you know nothing about her? How do you expect to convince everyone you're madly in love?'

'What's her favourite food? Her middle name? Her dream job?'

He was surprised to find he knew the answers. He had talked to Kat more than he'd ever talked to anyone. They'd shared plane journeys, car rides and dinners. They'd had hours alone together. She might have kept some secrets but he was convinced he knew the essence of her.

'Her favourite food is roast lamb but she will eat seafood any chance she gets, especially prawns. Her middle name is Maria, after her grandmother, and she always wanted to join the flying doctors but now, ultimately, she'd like to work with the air ambulance. Her favourite colour is red, her favourite movies are romantic comedies and her ex-fiancé's name is Adam.' They didn't need to know that he'd just learnt that but he'd give them what they want to hear even if it wasn't what they expected. 'She is kind and generous, warm-hearted, loving.'

Kat was all the things he'd never really experienced in one person before. The people he was normally surrounded by all had an agenda. Even if they were pleasant and honest they all needed something from him—a job, a favour, a photograph. He enjoyed Kat's company all the more because she seemed to enjoy his. She didn't expect things of him and she seemed to like him, the real him, not the movie star.

'I was raised to be hard-working and respectful. I like Kat and I respect her.' He avoided mentioning that he had nothing to do with his father and very little to do with his mother—he suspected that wouldn't win him any fans. In his opinion his family dynamics were irrelevant; he'd worked hard to become the man he was today, to have confidence in his abilities.

'I am a good person.' He wanted to be even

better. He wanted to be someone she would be proud of. He wanted to be someone who deserved someone like Kat in his life.

It was obvious Kat's family didn't think he was that person. They didn't think he was good enough and that bothered him. He would have to prove himself. To them and to Kat.

He wished Kat hadn't told her father the engagement was fake—maybe he'd be less hostile if he thought Oliver's intentions were honourable, but then again, maybe not. Either way, he doubted that Tony would be going to give a glowing recommendation of his new son-in-law-to-be if asked either.

'Family is the most important thing in her life,' Oliver said. 'She told me you and her mother were married for thirty-two years, and she wants that too.'

'And what if your little stunt stops her from getting that?'

'It won't. I promise this won't harm her reputation. I'll make sure that she is the one who calls off the engagement, that she comes out of this with her reputation intact.'

'How can you be sure?' Tony demanded. 'You're playing with her feelings. Her life. You should think carefully about what you are asking of her. Think about what she needs.'

He knew Tony was right. He needed to consider Kat's needs before his own but he didn't think that the fake engagement and Kat's needs were incompatible. They were both getting something out of the arrangement and he was positive they could do this without any repercussions.

Dinner was far from the relaxed Sunday night meal Kat was used to. The atmosphere was tense, everyone was on edge, and she wondered if she'd made a mistake agreeing to Oliver's request.

It was important to her that her family liked Oliver. It shouldn't matter—they weren't going to have a future together—but still, she hadn't expected this level of disapproval.

She, Saskia and Maya tried hard to keep the conversation flowing but it was difficult and there were plenty of uncomfortable silences. When Roger's phone rang in the middle of dinner, Kat jumped, startled by the shrill sound.

Roger got up to take the call but everyone could hear his half of the conversation and the tension increased as they waited to hear what had happened. It was clear there was an emergency of some sort. Dean was out of his seat before Roger disconnected the call.

'That was Emilia,' Roger said. 'Jimmy was

due home an hour ago and Emilia hasn't been able to get him on his cell phone.'

'What's going on?' Oliver asked Kat.

'Emilia's husband is a miner. Being late home and not answering his phone isn't unusual—phone reception can be dodgy out here—but he could have had an accident and she can't go and check on him because she doesn't know where he was working. That'll be why she called Roger. He knows where Jimmy's been working. He and Dean will go and take a look. Either Jimmy's phone has gone flat, is out of range, he's found opal or there's been a slide. An accident.'

'Is there anything I can do to help?'

'Not this time. The boys will raise the alarm if necessary. If there has been an accident the mine rescue team will be called in to help, and I need to be available. I'm going to have to take you back to the hotel, just in case.'

'Will you need your car?'

'No.'

'Why don't I borrow it? You don't need to drive me around. I can get myself home and that frees you up now. I will come back in the morning and pick you up—you're working on set tomorrow, right?'

Kat nodded. 'Are you sure?'

'Positive.'

'All right, I'll grab my keys.'

Kat waited while Oliver thanked Saskia and said goodbye to Rosa, Maya and her father. Her father was cool but at least he was acknowledging Oliver, although she was ashamed of the behaviour of the men in her family.

'I'm sorry about Papa—I didn't expect him to be quite so hostile,' she said as she and Oliver left the house.

'Don't worry about it. It doesn't matter if they don't like me as long as they don't make things difficult for you. Will you be OK?'

She nodded and stood outside the house and watched him drive away, wondering again if this would work out according to the plan.

She went inside to give Saskia and Maya a hand cleaning up.

'That went badly,' she said as she picked up a tea towel and started to dry the glasses.

'What did you expect?' Saskia asked.

'Why exactly did you agree to this?' asked Maya.

'He asked for my help.'

'And you couldn't refuse.'

'No, I couldn't. I owed him a favour. He got me back to Port Augusta after Papa's heart attack. He was amazing. So calm and in control. He did that for me and now I can do this for him.'

'What was so bad that he needed to create a good fake news story to deflect the bad news?'

Kat explained about the lawsuit. 'That's why I agreed to help him.'

'Your father will go ballistic if he hears about that.'

'That's why I'm not saying anything to Papa and the boys. Oliver is certain the lawsuit will be dropped and I believe him. They already don't trust him and I don't want to make things any worse.'

'You don't think they'll find out?'

'How? They never look at any entertainment news. They're only interested in three things—finding opal, the price of opal and the football.'

'And family,' Maya added as her phone beeped with a message. 'It's Roger,' she said. 'Jimmy's OK. He found a seam of opal and lost track of time.'

'Are you sure you're OK with this whole fake engagement?' Saskia asked; it was obvious she wasn't going to let this go. 'I know you like him. You don't feel like he's taking advantage of your generosity? Your feelings?'

'It's a business deal. It's not hurting anyone. I'm helping him. Just like he helped me and like he'll be helping the community with his donation to the drive-in and to the flying doctor.'

'It's one thing for him to help with a search or to donate money; it's another thing completely for him to get you involved in this publicity stunt. And what about going forwards? What's the plan then?'

'He'll win the lawsuit and then we'll call it off.'

'When will that be?'

'I'm not sure exactly.'

'And you're OK with that?'

Yes.' She'd have to be. It was the deal she'd made.

Kat scarcely had time to worry about her family's opinion of Oliver over the next week. Philippa had done her job and the video footage of Oliver's proposal had gone viral. The media had turned up in full force, clamouring for a story, and Kat's life had become a whirlwind of interviews and photo shoots interspersed between her work on and off set. It left barely any time for the two of them to be alone together and even less time for her to dwell on all the reasons her family disapproved of the 'engagement'.

She had explained Oliver's involvement in

getting her to Port Augusta from Adelaide to see her father, and she thought that maybe her Papa was softening a little, but it didn't really matter. It wasn't a real relationship. Her family didn't have to like him. It wouldn't bother Oliver, he didn't do family, and she wouldn't let it bother her.

They had done a couple of interviews early in the week, all arranged by Philippa, for the Australian media. Kat had been super-nervous but the journalists had been gentle and Oliver had been beside her all the time. He was very relaxed in front of the camera and his experience and calmness helped to settle Kat. Those interviews would be syndicated around the world but today they were faced with several interviews on a much larger scale. These would be the last of their joint interviews and first up was a panel of print journalists from the States followed by an interview that would go to air on American television.

Philippa had organised hair and make-up for Kat and she'd flown in a selection of outfits for Kat to choose from. Kat had insisted on Australian designers but she'd never heard of half of the ones Philippa had chosen. To give her credit, all the outfits were gorgeous but that made it impossible to choose just one. In the end Kat had asked Oliver's advice and he'd chosen a sleeveless cobalt-blue trouser suit with a halter neckline. The colour of the outfit reminded her of Oliver's eyes.

She felt overdressed, and over-made-up, for the middle of the morning but Oliver had reminded her that the television interview would be screened in the evening and she would look perfect.

He had held her hand and led her to the couch for the interview. He'd insisted that they be seated on a couch, not two separate chairs, and Kat had been grateful for that; she'd needed him close.

The interview began with all the questions Kat had become used to. How they had met. What Kat did for a job. How she had found growing up in Coober Pedy.

Oliver was very attentive: he was constantly touching her, his hand on her thigh, around her shoulders or holding her hand. He made her feel beautiful and she almost believed his answers when he talked about how they'd met, what he had thought when he first saw her and how they'd fallen in love. He almost had her convinced that he had real feelings for her but then she remembered that he did this all the time—put on a show for the media. He would give them what they wanted to keep himself in the headlines. It was all just an act. Even when he held her hand, a move that appeared so relaxed and natural, she noticed that he made sure her engagement ring was on show.

She forced herself to concentrate. This was their last interview and she had a part to play.

'Have you set a date for your wedding?'

'Not yet.' Oliver fielded most of the questions but he looked at her before answering, giving the impression that they were a team.

'Where will you get married?'

'We haven't decided.' He squeezed her hand and smiled at her and Kat knew the audience would think they had decided but were keeping that information to themselves.

'Will it be a big celebrity wedding or something private?'

'I'd like a big wedding. I want to show Kat off to everyone but she hasn't met my friends yet. It might be a small wedding if she doesn't like them.' His blue eyes sparkled as he laughed.

'Will they like her?'

'They will love her.' He looked at Kat, holding her gaze, his expression now earnest.

'Have you met her family?'

'I have.'

'And what did they think of Oliver, Kat?'

'They found him charming.' That was true of Maya and Saskia at least. Kat didn't feel she needed to be any more specific—in fact, Oliver had coached her in what to say.

'What about this lawsuit? You're standing by your man while he fights these charges, Kat?'

'Of course.'

'Any comment, Oliver?'

'No comment. I have every faith in our justice system. I am extremely sorry for the Hanson family's loss but we are focusing on our own future.'

'And what does that future look like, Kat? Will you be starting a family?' The journalist moved quickly along. Kat knew from previous interviews that they had to ask the question but, as it was all based on supposition, they couldn't really continue with that line. 'Do you want children?'

'Of course,' she replied, keeping her gaze directed at the journalist. 'Very much.' She couldn't look at Oliver; she was afraid he'd see the truth in her eyes.

'Oliver?'

'Definitely.'

He was looking at her and Kat's heart flipped in her chest. He looked as if he meant every word.

'The movie is about to wrap on location and

filming will move back to the States. Are you going to be moving too, Kat?'

'Kat will join me later. It won't be much fun for her in the States, away from her friends and family, while I'm working.'

Oliver was giving answers they hadn't discussed but Kat knew it didn't matter. None of this was real and by the time 'later' came around the lawsuit would be over and Oliver wouldn't need her any more. The idea was upsetting but there was nothing she could do.

Kat's heart sat like lead in her chest. It was supposed to be a party—it *was* a party—but she was miserable. The movie had wrapped on location and Oliver was leaving tomorrow. Filming would finish in the studio in the States. She knew she would miss him, she knew her life would never be the same without him. But she would cope, she'd have to.

She was talking to Julia when she saw him crossing the room towards them. It was getting late and she knew, at best, they only had a few hours left. She pasted a smile on her face, although her heart was breaking.

'Kat, could I borrow you for a second?'

He could have her for a lifetime if he wanted.

She nodded.

'I have something I want to give you,' he said as he took her arm and led her to a quiet corner. He sat her down and handed her a pile of beautifully wrapped gifts. A stack of box-shaped presents, but none small enough to be jewellery. They looked like books.

Kat swallowed her disappointment and opened the first one.

It was a photograph. He'd made copies of some of the publicity photos they had taken together. He'd framed them for her and included her favourite one. It captured her sitting on his lap. She was smiling and he was laughing. His head was thrown back, and they weren't look-ing at each other—she was leaning forwards away from him—but his arms were wrapped tightly around her waist, as if he was afraid to let her go. She wished that were the case.

Even though it was all an act she couldn't deny the photos were gorgeous. She looked happy; she glowed. She looked like a woman in love.

She hoped he didn't notice.

'These are gorgeous. Thank you.'

She knew she would treasure the pictures. One day. She wasn't sure if she was ready to display them just yet. She might need some time before she was ready to see his face every day, before she was ready to see the reflection of her unrequited love.

She hadn't meant to fall in love with him. She'd thought she'd be able to come out of this with her heart intact but it seemed fate had other ideas in store for her. It was time to bring this all to an end before she crumbled completely.

'Oliver?' she said as she wrapped the frames up again. She would look at them later. Alone. 'There's something I wanted to speak to you about. You're leaving tomorrow and I'm not sure what you and Philippa want me to do or say about our "engagement" once you're gone.'

'I thought maybe I'd say you're coming to visit me in a few weeks. What do you think?'

She didn't want to visit. She wasn't interested in a holiday. This was her chance to find out if he had genuine feelings for her at all. She wanted him to offer her a future. A life together. She wanted him to propose to her for real. But it seemed a few more days was all she could have. It wasn't enough, not nearly, and she wouldn't settle for that. 'Is that necessary? Don't you think the lawsuit might be resolved by then?'

'That wouldn't matter. You could still visit me.'

She shook her head. She'd hoped she wouldn't

be faced with this scenario, the one where Oliver didn't profess his undying love, but she'd thought this through, just in case. 'We have to call the engagement off eventually. It will make our break-up more authentic if we don't see each other again after you leave. I thought we could go with the story that I am staying here while my dad recovers. When the lawsuit is over your life will go back to normal. You won't need me any more. You'll forget all about me.'

She waited for him to say that wasn't what he wanted.

'You don't want to visit me?' he said, which wasn't the same thing at all.

'I wouldn't want to leave Papa.'

'Kat, he's fine. He's recovered well from his surgery. You could leave for a few weeks.'

She felt guilty using her father as her excuse but she wanted more than a few weeks. She wasn't going to settle for less even if it meant suffering a broken heart. She knew that if he loved her they would find a way to work things out. But it looked as if she wasn't going to get her wish. 'I have to stay.'

'If that's what you want.'

No. It wasn't what she wanted at all. She wanted him to say he loved her, that he couldn't live without her, that he would stay with her. But she knew that was impossible. 'I should go,' she said. She didn't belong here. In his world.

'Now?'

She nodded. She loved him but she didn't expect him to love her back. She needed to make a clean break. She couldn't stand the thought of saying goodbye but she knew she had to. And she had to do it quickly.

They didn't speak as he walked with her to her car. There was nothing left to say.

He took her in his arms and spun her to face him. 'You are wrong, by the way,' he said as he lifted her chin and looked into her eyes. 'I'll never forget you,' he said as his lips came down onto hers.

The kiss was gentle. Sad. Kat didn't know that was even possible.

She knew it was a goodbye kiss but she thought it might be better called the 'break my heart' kiss.

'You have an open invitation to visit me any time, so let me know if you change your mind,' he said as she made herself let go of him.

She nodded and got into her car. She could feel tears threatening to spill and she didn't want to cry in front of him. She didn't want him to see how her heart was breaking.

She wiped away her tears with the back of her hand as she drove away. She didn't look back. She knew she'd turn right around if she did.

He watched her drive away. He could scarcely breathe and his heart ached in his chest. He wasn't ready to say goodbye. He wanted to chase after her, to beg her to reconsider but he knew he'd be wasting his time. She wasn't going to leave her father. Her family came first. It was what she had always told him but he'd hoped that maybe he would be worth the sacrifice on her part. But if she wouldn't leave for a few weeks, how could he ask her to leave for ever?

And how did he expect it to work? What would they do going forwards? Where did he see them? Did they have a future? Could he expect her to leave everything she loved behind to travel with him? To live his nomadic existence…his lonely, nomadic existence? He couldn't ask her to leave with him. Everything she loved was here. Her family, her career, her world. She was surrounded by people who loved her. And she had chosen to stay with them. He'd known she would but he'd hoped differently.

He wanted her to love him, to choose him, but was that fair? Did he love her?

He didn't know. He'd never been in love before. All he knew was that, watching her drive away, he felt as if she was taking his heart with her.

He stood and watched until her tail lights disappeared.

Leaving him alone again. As always.

CHAPTER NINE

'HOW ARE YOU? Have you heard from him?' Saskia asked as she sat on Kat's bed and watched her tidy her room.

'No.'

Oliver had been gone for a week. Kat had seen an interview he'd given at Sydney Airport as he left the country. He'd been asked about his fiancée and he had looked suitably upset when he'd replied that Kat was staying in Coober Pedy temporarily while her father was recovering from surgery but was planning to join him later.

She knew that wouldn't happen.

'You should have gone with him.'

'I can't leave Papa. I'm all he has.'

'It's not for ever, Kat. And that's not true. He has Rosa, me, the boys, Maya. We're all here. You could have gone.'

'What would be the point? It's not real, Sas. It's all make-believe.' Oliver had asked her to visit but Kat wanted more. She wanted for ever. She wanted true love.

Saskia picked up a framed photo. Kat's favourite. 'It looks pretty real.'

'It was all an act.' At least on his part. She wanted to believe they shared something real but she really wasn't sure. She'd fallen in love with him and their connection had felt real to her, but what if she'd fallen for Oliver because of a fantasy? Because she'd always dreamt of finding the one. What if he wasn't the one but was simply an option? 'He doesn't need me.'

'Are you sure? You could go and find out. What's the worst thing that could happen? You find it's not what you thought and you come home miserable. You're already miserable, so isn't it better to take a chance? What are you afraid of?'

She was afraid he wouldn't want her. That she wasn't sophisticated enough and wouldn't have anything in common with his life. His friends. His world. That she wouldn't belong. That she'd look out of place and he'd see she wasn't right for him.

She was afraid that their differences were bigger than their similarities because, after all, what did they really have in common? They had talked and laughed and loved. They had shared secrets and dreams, but those secrets and dreams were so different.

She felt as if she knew him but she was scared to take a chance. It was easier to stay than to take a risk. She liked to play it safe. She liked to follow rules. She liked routine. He was a rule-breaker, independent. She needed her family and friends. He was a loner. She could get past all those differences with the exception of family. She wasn't sure if she could be with someone who didn't value family.

'We are too different.'

'Don't be ridiculous.' Saskia wasn't holding back with her opinion. 'Since when do you think that every couple has to be exactly alike? Why should they think alike, act alike? Imagine how boring that would be. Think about how he makes you feel.'

He made her feel special. He made her feel beautiful. He made her happy. And now he'd made her miserable. She was lonely. She missed him.

'If you're not going to go to him maybe you just need to get away from here for a while. Away from the memories. We should have a girls' trip. Maya and I could leave the kids with our husbands and go with you. What do you think?'

'Maybe,' she said, but what she thought was, what if she was away and something else went wrong? Or, even worse, what if Oliver came back for her but she wasn't here?

She knew that was a ridiculous notion but she could admit, if only to herself, that it was what she was dreaming of.

She'd fallen in love with him but there was nothing she could do.

He was gone. It was over.

Kat looked at the clock. Fifteen minutes until the end of her shift.

Her life had been dragging on painfully slowly for the past four weeks since Oliver had left. Every morning she woke up hoping to feel better. Hoping she wouldn't feel as though part of her was missing. When would it end?

'Do you think it's safe to get changed now?' she asked Dave. 'Saskia and Maya are going to collect me from here.'

She was going out to dinner with her cousins' wives to celebrate Maya's birthday. The other crew would be here to take over shortly and she wanted to be ready to go, but she knew how often a last-minute emergency would derail any plans for an on-time knock-off.

'Sure. It's been—'

'Don't say it!' Kat held up her hand in warning. She was superstitious enough to stop Dave from uttering the word. The minute you said a shift had been quiet, chaos would descend.

Dave laughed. 'Go and get changed. I'll hold the fort.'

Kat barely had time to get her boots off before Dave was knocking at the door. 'Kat, we've got a call-out. Are you still dressed?'

She sighed and stuffed her feet back into her boots, leaving her bag with her change of clothes behind.

'Take your bag with us,' Dave said. 'I might be able to drop you straight to dinner.'

She doubted that—it seemed as though everything that could go wrong did. Her life was a mess. 'Where are we going?' she asked as they climbed into the ambulance.

'Out towards Crocodile Harry's place,' he said as he handed her the GPS coordinates so she could punch them into the satnav as he drove. 'A couple of tourists; one's had a fall, a suspected fractured leg.'

Crocodile Harry's was only ten minutes out of town. It was where George had filmed the cave scenes and the mention of it made Kat immediately think of Oliver.

'Do we know what we're looking for?' Kat asked.

'A white Toyota Landcruiser.'

Lucky, then, they had the GPS details. Those vehicles were a dime a dozen out here.

Dave drove west into the setting sun. Kat flipped the sun visor down, the sun was low in the sky making visibility difficult, and her sunglasses weren't providing enough resistance against the glare as she searched the horizon.

'I see a car.' She pointed to their left, to where a four-by-four sat on top of a hill. It was approximately in the right position according to the satnav.

Dave turned off the main road and bumped his way over the rough terrain. As they approached Kat could see a table and chairs set up beside the vehicle. It looked as if someone had gone to a lot of trouble to set up a picnic to watch the sunset. Four tall posts had been erected and fairy lights were strung between them. Solar powered, they were just beginning to shine in the dusk. The table and two chairs sat beneath the lights.

Kat jumped out of the ambulance, swung open the back door and grabbed her kit. She headed for the vehicle.

A man appeared from below the crest of the hill. The way he moved reminded her of Oliver and she felt a pang of loss as she blocked that thought. She had been thinking of him on the drive out here and now her imagination was playing tricks on her.

The man came closer. He looked just like Oliver.

She held her hand up to shield her face from the setting sun. Surely it couldn't be him?

'Hello, Kat.'

It was him. The sound of his voice set her heart racing. He smiled his familiar smile; it started at one corner of his mouth, spreading across his lips and lighting up his eyes. Kat couldn't breathe. She felt dizzy and was afraid her legs would buckle.

'Oliver? What are you doing here?'

'Waiting for you.'

She looked around in confusion. 'Where's the patient?'

'There isn't one.'

She turned around to question Dave, unable to work out what was going on. Dave stood behind her holding the bag that contained her change of clothes. Clothes she had packed to wear to dinner with Saskia and Maya. He passed the bag to her, swapping it for the medical kit, and walked off without a word.

'I don't understand,' she said, turning back to Oliver. 'I'm supposed to be having dinner with Saskia.'

He was shaking his head. 'You don't have

any other plans. Dave, Saskia, Maya—they're all part of this.'

'Part of what?'

'Come and sit down.' He took her hand and Kat clung to him, not sure she was going to be able to walk without help. Her brain had frozen. Nothing made sense.

Oliver pulled out a chair for her at the table and she almost collapsed into the seat. The table had been covered with a white table-cloth, and two champagne glasses, an ice bucket with a bottle of champagne and a vase of flowers had been laid out on top. She stared at the tableau.

'Did you do this?'

He nodded. 'I did it for you. There's something I need to discuss with you. It's about our engagement. There's something I need.'

'I'm sorry, I should have thought,' she said as she started to tug at her engagement ring. Her hands were hot and clammy, the ring tight on her finger. It wouldn't budge.

She wasn't sure why she was still wearing it. It was totally impractical in her job but she hadn't been able to make herself take it off. She pretended she was worried she might lose it but that wasn't true. She wore it because it was a reminder of him. She'd been surprised that he had never asked for it back, but then they'd never officially called off the engagement. She supposed this was it.

But that didn't explain the champagne, the flowers, the table under the lights. She was totally confused.

'What are you doing?' he asked her as she continued her futile attempt to remove the ring.

'Of course, you need this back.' She reached into the ice bucket and grabbed some ice cubes to cool down her finger.

'What? No! That's not what I came for. You can keep it.'

'I don't want it,' she said as she finally tugged it free. 'You need to give it back to Philippa.'

'I suppose I should,' he said as he took it and slipped it into his pocket. 'You never liked it anyway.'

He was right, she hadn't, not only because it was impractical but also because it had no meaning. It hadn't been given with love.

'It's a beautiful ring,' she said, 'but it was never mine to keep. I know we need to end our engagement but you didn't need to come all the way back here.' Oliver had been in touch a week ago to tell her the lawsuit had been dropped. She'd known then that he didn't need her any more. 'I could have sent the ring back to you.'

'I'm not here for the ring, Kat. I'm here for you.'

'For me?'

He nodded. 'I never should have left. I should have fought for you. For us. I should have told you I love you.'

'You love me?'

'I do.'

It was exactly what she'd wanted to hear but she couldn't understand why he hadn't told her this before. What had changed? What was going on? 'Why didn't you tell me this before?'

'I was scared.'

'Of what?'

'I didn't think I deserved you. I didn't think you would choose me. I thought you would choose your family. I know how important they are to you and I didn't know how I could compete with them, but then I realised I don't want it to be a competition. I don't want you to choose them or me. I want you to choose me as well. I want to be your family too. I just hope I'm not too late.

'I want to be the man you deserve, the man you love. I want you to be proud of me. You have given me a sense of purpose—you have made me want to be a better version of myself. A better person, a better son, a better man. But I had to work out who I was. Who I wanted to be.'

'I don't understand.'

'Let me explain.' He reached across the table and held her hand. 'I don't think I have ever really felt comfortable in my skin. I have never truly felt a part of something; I've always felt as though I'm a disappointment. I think that's why I love acting—it's a chance to escape from myself, from reality. It's a chance to be someone different, someone who isn't real, someone who won't disappoint real people. For years I've been searching, trying to find my place in the world, trying to work out what my purpose is, but it's been a lonely existence. But since I met you I can see myself as part of a bigger picture. Part of something special.

'I want to be part of something real. You exist in the real world and you've shared your world with me, you've shown me what is out there. I'm tired of make-believe—I want to be part of your world. Of your life. I love you and I want to marry you.'

'You want to marry me?'

'I do. I love you and I want to spend my life with you. Until I met you I didn't believe that there could be one person who was the right fit for me, or that I would be the right person for somebody either. I thought that sounded cliché, boring, that there would be nothing left to look forward to, but you have shown me that with the right person I can have all of that and more. I can have someone to share that with. Something to look forward to together. I want to be part of something bigger than myself. I want to be part of us. Everything about you has made me change my mind. I'm a changed man. Trite maybe, clichéd certainly, but that doesn't mean it isn't true. I want to be the man you want to spend the rest of your life with. I need you.'

The sun had set now. It was nearing winter and the end of the day came quickly in the desert. The temperature was dropping as darkness fell. The sky was dark and clear and the fairy lights merged together with the stars.

'I wanted to bring you out here so it was just you and me this time. This is about us. Just us. I want you to know this is real. There's no performance. No agenda. I know you think we are very different but there is one thing we have in common: we both want to be loved. I love you and I hope that, just maybe, you love me too.'

He stood and knelt in the red earth beside Kat. 'Katarina Maria Angelis, I love you, I adore you, I need you. I want to spend the rest of my life with you, as your husband. Please will you make my life complete? Will you marry me?'

'Yes,' she said as she pulled him to his feet. 'I do love you and I do adore you. I need you too and yes, I will marry you.'

She wound her arms around his neck and kissed him deeply, pouring all her emotions into the kiss, letting him know that she loved him, adored him and needed him.

'There's one more thing,' he said as he pulled a ring box from his pocket. He held it in the palm of his hand and flipped the lid open. A round black opal was nestled inside. Even in the semi-darkness it flashed with vibrant colours—red, blue and green. It was in a bezel setting, surrounded by diamonds. Kat didn't recognise the setting but she was sure she recognised the stone. Black opals were extremely rare.

'Is that my mother's opal?'

Oliver nodded. 'Your father said you've always loved it. He gave it to me and I got it reset today.'

'My father gave this to you?'

'Yes. Along with his blessing. I went to see him, to explain my intentions. I wanted him to believe that I deserve you. I wanted him to trust that I am worthy of marrying his daughter. That I will take care of you. That I love you.'

He slipped the ring onto her finger. It was perfect.

He was perfect.

And, as he kissed her again, Kat knew they would be perfect together.

* * * * *